Love Inspired SUSPENSE

HAZARDOUS HOLIDAY

Liz Johnson

D0034869

MEN OF VALOR

Love Inspired
SUSPENSE

Suspenseful romances of danger and faith.

AVAILABLE THIS MONTH

ROOKIE K-9 UNIT CHRISTMAS
Rookie K-9 Unit
Lenora Worth and
Valerie Hansen

CLASSIFIED CHRISTMAS MISSION
Wrangler's Corner
Lynette Eason

CHRISTMAS CONSPIRACY
First Responders
Susan Sleeman

STALKING SEASON
Smoky Mountain Secrets
Sandra Robbins

HAZARDOUS HOLIDAY
Men of Valor
Liz Johnson

MISTLETOE REUNION THREAT
Rangers Under Fire
Virginia Vaughan

ISBN-13: 978-0-373-44786-2

EAN

"It's okay," Zach said. "It's going to be okay."

But his words didn't make the hail of bullets stop.

And then he heard the sweet song of police sirens. And just like that, as quickly as they'd started, the shots ended.

He released Kristi just enough for her to look up at him, eyes wild and curls askew. She dropped her gaze to her son and cupped his cheeks in her palms. "Are you all right?"

Cody looked mildly shell-shocked but shrugged anyway. "I'm okay."

She turned her arm, and Zach saw a red swath from her elbow to her shoulder. Grabbing her with less finesse and more fear, he said, "I thought you said you weren't hit."

Kristi followed his gaze to the smear of blood and frowned, looking puzzled. "It's not me. I'm not..." Her eyes widened in alarm when she looked at his shoulder. "Oh, Zach."

She scrambled to pull off her sweater and pressed it against his arm.

Pain seared through him like a flash of lightning. It was as if his entire arm was on fire, and he hadn't even noticed. Only now could he feel the blood rolling down to his elbow.

But at least it was his and not hers.

By day **Liz Johnson** is a marketing manager at a Christian publisher. She makes time to write late at night and is a two-time ACFW Carol Award finalist. She lives in Nashville and enjoys exploring local music and theater, and she makes frequent trips to Arizona to dote on her nieces and nephews. She writes stories filled with heart, humor and happily-ever-afters and can be found online at www.lizjohnsonbooks.com.

Books by Liz Johnson

Love Inspired Suspense

Men of Valor

A Promise to Protect
SEAL Under Siege
Navy SEAL Noel
Navy SEAL Security
Hazardous Holiday

Witness Protection

Stolen Memories

The Kidnapping of Kenzie Thorn
Vanishing Act
Code of Justice

Visit the Author Profile page at Harlequin.com.

HAZARDOUS HOLIDAY

LIZ JOHNSON

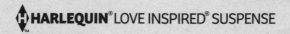

HARLEQUIN® LOVE INSPIRED® SUSPENSE

LOVE INSPIRED BOOKS

Recycling programs for this product may not exist in your area.

ISBN-13: 978-0-373-44786-2

Hazardous Holiday

www.Harlequin.com

Printed in U.S.A.

To everything there is a season,
and a time to every purpose under the heaven.
—Ecclesiastes 3:1

For the readers.
May you continue to find joy in stories
and hope in the greatest story of all.

PROLOGUE

"I guess we'd better get married, then."

At Zach's words, Kristi Tanner dropped her mug. It shattered and splashed coffee across her kitchen floor, dousing the nearby cabinets in the pale, creamy drink.

All six feet two inches of Zach McCloud stooped in silence to scoop up the porcelain shards, but she couldn't move as his words rang in her ears, over and over.

We'd better get married, then.

Get married, then.

Married.

As proposals went, that was the very worst one she'd ever heard. Of course, she'd heard only two in person. But this was nothing like a sweet, romantic scene from the movies.

From his knees, Zach stared up at her. "I guess that was a bit of a surprise."

She gave him a curt nod.

"Sorry about that." He threw the broken mug away, then shifted into the traditional proposal pose. She sucked in a quick gasp. Was he going to do it right this time?

But she didn't know what *right* looked like.

When Aaron had asked her to marry him, he'd pulled a ring out of the front pocket of his work jeans and slipped it on her finger before she'd even known what was happening. That had been fine with her, since she'd been in love with Aaron Tanner since he shared his pudding cup with her in the second grade.

But he was never going to share his dessert with her again.

Tears burned her eyes, and she tried to wipe them away. No matter how similar their hazel-green eyes and cleft chins—genetic traits the cousins shared—the man kneeling before her wasn't Aaron.

"Why *exactly* do you think we should get married?"

Zach rubbed at his bald head, the superclose shave most likely masking the McCloud men's tendency toward early hair loss. "Guess I sort of jumped ahead there."

"You think?" She couldn't help the snark that laced her words. It wasn't pointed at him precisely. It wasn't pointed anywhere actually.

Maybe a little at Aaron.

Definitely kind of at Aaron.

He'd promised they'd grow old together working the ranch they both loved.

Then he'd gone and walked in on a robbery in progress. He'd tried to protect the pregnant clerk behind the gas station counter. And he'd been shot three times in the chest.

How dare he leave her to raise their five-year-old son, Cody, all by herself?

"As I see it, you can't stay in Montana," he said, his voice low, laced with pain that was entirely too familiar.

Aaron hadn't just been Zach's cousin. He'd been his best friend, too.

He snagged a towel from the counter and mopped up the coffee streaks down the cabinets before wiping at the puddle on the floor. "Not with Cody's condition."

That was a placid euphemism for the sinister heart defect that had been slowly stealing her son's life, breath by breath.

"He needs to be near the best doctors when he reaches the top of the transplant list. And you need support... and insurance." The flecks of brown in his green eyes seemed to glow as he leaned forward. "You're all alone out here."

Like she needed the reminder. Their nearest neighbor was more than a dozen miles away. The nearest hospital was more than fifty miles. Aaron's parents—Zach's aunt and uncle—had moved into town when she and Aaron took over the ranch.

And the ranch hands spent their time mending fences and minding the herd. They weren't around the house, if she ever needed them.

But why would she need them? She'd grown up on a ranch—albeit a much smaller spread. Still, she could stitch up a cut, round up a stray and fix a broken tractor.

If something happened to her, she'd get through.

But now that something had happened to Cody, well, she'd go crazy if she couldn't get him to help fast enough.

On paper, Zach's solution made sense. But in reality... could she really do this? Could she marry Zach McCloud?

Zach stared up into the deepest brown eyes he'd ever known and called himself every kind of fool for springing his plan on Kristi. In all the time he'd spent chewing on the idea—since he'd heard about Cody's heart condition—he should have had time to come up with a better approach. But despite her shock, he still knew this was the right decision.

He'd even asked his pastor for advice. They'd spent two hours searching Scripture for direction.

Time and again they'd landed in the book of James and the command to care for the orphans and widows.

He could care for her and help her.

Marrying her was the best way he knew to do it.

And if he'd been in love with her since they were sixteen, well, he wouldn't let that get in the way of being the friend she needed, the friend Aaron would expect him to be.

Focusing on Kristi, he narrowed his gaze and dropped his voice. "It makes sense."

She blinked rapidly, a motion he knew well. She was fighting the tears that threatened to spill. He guessed they came pretty regularly nowadays.

But she didn't say no. So he plowed forward.

"Look, I know it's strange. But Aaron was practically my brother. I'd do anything for him. Which means I'd do anything for you and Cody." Zach rubbed his head. "If we get married, you'll be taken care of. You'll have the navy's best insurance. You'll have a place to live in San Diego, close to some of the best pediatric transplant surgeons in the country."

"But we haven't spent any time together since high school."

They'd all spent every summer together when they were kids, but Zach had joined the navy right out of high school and hadn't been back to Montana in years. She probably remembered him as a shy, gangly tenth grader.

He wasn't that kid anymore.

Just as he was formulating his case, she shook her

head firmly. "I can't. I'm not ready to be married to someone else. It's only been a year."

Fifteen months to be exact, but he wouldn't argue the point. She wasn't ready to share her life with another man. Maybe she never would be. But that wasn't what he was offering.

"I have a three-bedroom town house. There's more than enough room for you and Cody to each have your own. And…and my team is being deployed."

"Deployed? Where?"

He shook his head. She might as well get used to it. He didn't talk about where his SEAL team served. Ever.

But her frown said that wasn't acceptable. "When?"

"In about four weeks. For a year."

Her eyes narrowed, and she crossed her arms over her chest. "You're suggesting I leave everything and everyone I know and move to San Diego. But you're not going to be there."

He stood, towering over her, but she didn't step back.

"I know it's not ideal, but I don't have a better suggestion." He rubbed the back of his neck as he hung his head. "I want to help. And all I'm asking in return is that you trust me."

"And how long will I be in San Diego?"

"As long as you and Cody need it." He shrugged. "You have a home there for as long as it takes."

"What about after?"

He mouthed the word *after* and twisted the towel in his hands until the fibers strained. After Cody's surgery? After she didn't need him anymore? He had no answers, but still a strong conviction that this was what he was supposed to do.

"We'll figure it out."

"Momma?"

Her gaze swung to the kitchen entry, and Zach followed it a second behind. The little boy looked smaller than his five years, practically skin and bones, his face dominated by his dad's big green eyes.

"What are you doing out of bed?" Reaching out a hand to him, she said, "Come here, little man." He ran to her and wrapped his arms around her waist, tucking his face into her side as she sifted her fingers through his sandy-blond hair.

Before she could make introductions, he squatted in front of them. Eye level with the boy, Zach held out his hand. "You must be Cody. I'm Zach. I've heard a lot of great things about you. Your dad talked about you all the time."

For an instant Cody's lips trembled. "You knew my daddy?"

Zach's eyes burned. "He was my very best friend and the best man I knew."

A sniff from above drew Zach's attention, and he looked up in time to see Kristi wiping her face.

"All right."

Was that a *yes* to his proposal—botched though it may have been?

She seemed to read his question on his face and nodded slowly. "Bud, how would you like to live by the ocean?"

ONE

Thirteen months later

Kristi Tanner had been an idiot.

There was no other word for it.

What on earth had possessed her to marry a man she barely knew and to move into an unfamiliar neighborhood? She still didn't feel safe here, even after more than a year. Though that sense of danger mostly stemmed from the brown sedan that had been parked across the street from her town house on and off for two weeks. It didn't seem to belong to a single one of her neighbors.

She gave it another hard look as the vehicle pulled past for the hundredth time.

She couldn't be the only one in the neighborhood who noticed the strange drive-bys or felt like someone was watching her unload groceries and pull weeds.

Maybe that was all part of life in a big city. Maybe she should have expected the weight of a hundred eyes on her. Only it hadn't started until a few weeks ago. Right after the scene at her office.

She shook her head. She didn't have time today to think about the odd shiver down her back or that silly car. Not when she was expected at the base.

When Zach had shipped out, a year had seemed so long. He'd been gone, and she and Cody had built their life in San Diego. Doctor's appointments. A new job. Cody's homeschooling. Birthdays and holidays. They'd made the most of them all, every day grieving their loss a little less.

But now Zach was coming back—coming home.

To her home.

"What time do they get in?"

Cody sagged in the backseat, but his smile couldn't be denied. Despite his pale lips and sallow skin, his eyes danced with anticipation. And Kristi couldn't deny him his joy at the prospect of seeing his longtime pen pal.

Not even if her insides were a knot of nerves.

"His flight was supposed to arrive at one."

"Hurry." He kicked at the back of her seat as his voice rose. "We're going to be late."

The light changed, and she zipped in front of a red sports car, headed toward the Coronado Bridge. "We're not going to be late. And stop kicking my seat."

"Yes, Momma." The frantic beats at her back ended immediately. "But hurry?" he pleaded.

She took a corner a little faster than she'd anticipated, and her purse flew across the passenger seat, sending several worn envelopes flying to the floorboard. She'd carried Zach's letters with her every day since they began arriving. One every month. All written in a bold, blocky hand.

They weren't filled with flowery poetry or sweet words. They never hinted at affection or the pain of distance.

No one would dare to classify them as love letters.

Still, they offered a peek into the heart of the man

she'd married. Funny stories of his team's time abroad. Concern for Cody. Scriptures he'd been reading.

She'd pored over them all.

And never sent a single response.

It was so much easier to tag a note on to the end of Cody's emails, letting Zach know they were well and his house was fine, than to put her real thoughts on to paper. Her real doubts.

At first she'd wondered every day after their court-house ceremony if she'd made the right decision. But as the weeks ticked by, life had settled into a new normal.

Until the call a few days ago.

Ashley Waterstone, the wife of the senior chief of Zach's SEAL team, had called with news. The team was coming home.

"Momma?"

"Yes, Cody?"

"Where's Zach going to stay?"

Her stomach clenched, her grip on the wheel turning her knuckles white. As promised, Zach's three-bedroom home was big enough for all of them, but it would be strange to have another person in the space she'd come to see as hers and Cody's.

"Because I was thinking he could stay in my room."

Kristi couldn't hold back a giggle.

"I have bunk beds, and he could have the top one." Cody met her gaze in the rearview mirror and smiled broadly. "Do you think he'd want to?"

"Well, bud," she said as tactfully as she could, "he's been working hard for a long time. He might need lots of good sleep."

Cody shook his head vigorously. "I bet he'll want to. I'll ask him. My Chevy night-light is really cool."

"That it is. You ask him. But if he says no, then you say okay. Okay?"

"Okay."

They turned left and then followed the road through the lush greenery beneath a cloudless blue sky. The sun shone off the legendary red spires of the Hotel del Coronado to their right. Another sunny-and-seventy day in Southern California, even in December.

Of all the familiar things she missed about Montana— her friends, Aaron's family and the beauty of Big Sky Country—she never missed the winter weather.

As she pulled up to the gatehouse at the entrance to the base, Cody began chanting his excitement. When she rolled her window down, the guard looked into the backseat at the ruckus.

"Is someone's dad coming home today?" the big man asked.

Kristi swallowed the lump in her throat. The same one that seemed to pop up at the oddest reminders of Aaron. "I'm Kristi T—McCloud. I'm here to pick up Zach."

The man's eyes grew bright as he looked at her driver's license. "Ziggy? Oh, he's here. In their offices probably." He quickly handed back her license and gave her directions to a trailer.

She repeated them to herself over and over. "Left, right, across from the third pier."

The building wasn't much, marked only with a number and a few big trucks in the parking spaces beside it.

She pulled into a spot and took a deep breath. She could do this. Things were going to change, but it didn't have to be for the worse. They'd already survived one adjustment. They could get through another. With a firm nod of her head and a silent prayer heavenward, she opened her door, then helped Cody out of the backseat.

Just as Cody's feet hit the ground, a small white SUV flew into the spot two over. A gorgeous brunette tumbled out from behind the wheel. She sprinted for the door to the trailer, and it slammed closed behind her.

Cody looked confused, his little eyes squinting against the sun.

"I think we're in the right place," Kristi reassured him. "Someone is excited to see her husband. Are you excited to see Zach?"

"Yes." He pumped his fist in the air as best he could, and she ushered him toward the building, holding open the door as he ambled in.

Compared with the bright sun, the fluorescent interior lights were almost black, and she had to blink quickly. As soon as her eyes adjusted, she spotted the same brunette from outside, swinging around the neck of a man in brown camouflage. His arms locked around her waist, his eyes closed as they spun.

"Miss me?" he asked, and she replied with a kiss.

Kristi suddenly felt very out of place. Maybe they should go wait in the car. Or drive over the bridge and wait for Zach to show up at the house. This was a time for sweet reunions between real loves, not awkward embraces with faux wives.

But just as she snagged Cody's arm, a familiar voice made her insides tremble. It was low and filled with concern.

"Kristi?"

Cody wiggled free and ran for Zach, who easily scooped the thin boy into his arms. Zach's smile was genuine but surprised as he patted Cody's back and ruffled his hair.

"Good to see you, little man."

Cody threw his skinny arms over the broad shoulders and hugged Zach's neck like they were best friends. "You came back!"

"Told you I would."

"And you're in time for Christmas!"

"You don't say." Zach's smile faltered as he looked in her direction and caught her gaze.

Embarrassment washed over her for no particular reason, and she wrapped her arms around her middle.

The corner of Zach's eyes crinkled as his gaze dropped to the floor, and she felt every inch of his survey. He stepped closer and leaned in, his warmth wrapping around her. "Good to see you." He pressed his lips to her cheek, and her nerves prickled to life, down her neck and right into her already-seasick stomach.

The best she could manage in response was a trembling smile.

"The transplant coordinator says I'm almost at the top of the list."

She thanked God for Cody every day. And especially when his random outburst drew all of Zach's attention and a big grin.

"How're you feeling?"

Cody shrugged, wilting into Zach's shoulder. "Tired mostly. Momma makes me take a break every day. Even when Mrs. Drummond is staying with me while mom's at work."

Zach laughed, a rich baritone that reverberated off the fake-wood walls, at Cody's euphemism for naps. "I might be able to match you break for break, man. I haven't gotten a full night of sleep in a while…"

"What were you doing?"

"Cody, no," she interrupted. "Don't ask—"

"I was protecting people who can't protect themselves."

Cody's eyes filled with sadness, and the pout of his lower lip quivered. "Did their daddies die, too?"

With a flash of the same sadness in his own eyes, Zach nodded. "Some of them."

"Then I'm glad you went to help them." Just like that, Cody assessed that Zach's work was worthy, and he moved on to the next topic of interest, pointing at the embracing couple. "Who are they?"

Zach turned to look behind him. "That's Willie G.—I mean, Will Gumble and his wife, Jess. And that's the senior chief." A tall, lean man stepped out of an office and walked up to them, holding out his hand to shake Kristi's.

"Matt Waterstone. You must be Kristi. Zig talks about you all the time."

A truck full of gravel emptied into her stomach, and she barely managed to shake his hand before her knees began trembling. What had Zach been saying about her? Did they all know she'd been forced to marry a man she didn't love for the sake of her son? Her hands shook, and she wrung them in front of her, trying not to be intimidated by the steel in his posture.

Zach grunted his disagreement but didn't get out a word before the door flung open and three towheaded kids raced inside. They shouted and cheered as Matt squatted before them, scooping even the oldest—probably seven or eight—into his arms.

Each child was given a hard kiss on the forehead before Ashley, their mom, arrived. The kids seemed to know the drill, and they parted ways as she reached her husband and held him tightly.

Kristi took several shuffling steps backward. She

didn't belong here. Not with these real family reunions. Grabbing for Cody's hand, she snagged Zach's bare forearm instead, and they both jumped at the contact.

"I'm sorry." Her voice barely carried, but the firm shake of his head told her he'd heard her just fine.

"Are you ready to go home?" he asked.

She looked away. "Anytime."

"Let me get my bag."

When she reached for Cody, the boy whimpered and tucked his head into Zach's neck. Kristi flinched. "I'm sorry. He's really tired. This is usually one of his rest times."

Zach didn't quite smile, but there was a tenderness in his eyes as he readjusted the weight in his arm. "No problem. I'll be right back."

True to his word, Zach ducked into an office and returned in less than a minute. The large camouflage bag slung over his shoulder was bigger than her son, but he carried both without any indication of the burden. With a wave to his fully occupied teammates, he ushered her into the bright sunlight and to the car.

Usually she had to wrestle Cody into his seat when he was on the verge of sleep, but Zach made it look easy. And with his bag stowed in the trunk, he looked from the driver's door to her hands to her face. "Want me to drive?"

"Oh." Her gaze dropped to the faintly jingling keys in her trembling fingers. That's right. She didn't have to drive all the time now. She wasn't alone anymore. Even if she didn't know quite what that meant. "Sure. That would be nice."

When she climbed into the passenger side, she had another reason to be grateful she'd passed over the keys. His letters were still strewn across the floorboard, and she scrambled to collect them and shove them into her oversize purse before he noticed.

Zach couldn't seem to take his eyes off her, even as he pulled off the base and toward the bridge.

He'd never had a welcoming party before. His mom and dad had tried to meet him following his first deployment, but after his team had been delayed and then called back to duty, they'd headed back to Texas. This was new. And not unpleasant.

"You didn't have to be here today." His tone came out thicker, gruffer than he'd intended, and her eyes flashed wide.

"Should we not have come? I didn't know what you'd want, and we didn't realize—"

He held up his hand quickly to cut her off while he cleared his throat. "No. I'm glad you did. I just wasn't expecting it. You didn't have to."

Kristi's head dipped, her hair falling over her shoulder and blocking his view of her face. "Ashley called and told me to be here. I thought maybe you'd asked her to get in touch with us."

His stomach gave an involuntary jerk, and he pressed a fist to his knee. He should have thought to do that. He'd just never had a family in San Diego before. Not even an unconventional one.

"I guess we both have some adjusting to do."

She heaved a little sigh that sounded as tightly wound as he was. And in some strange way, it helped to know that he wasn't the only one unsure how to navigate this new terrain.

As he pulled her little green four-door onto the bridge, a large black van came up behind them. He watched it through the rearview, its bulk taking up most of his mirror and making the hairs on his arms stand up. It was following them awfully closely.

He frowned but kept his speed up, shifting into the middle lane of the eastbound traffic. The van stayed put, and he let out a slow breath.

"Cody's been so excited to see you. He told the checker at the grocery store that his SEAL was coming home. I think she thought you were a pet."

Zach chuckled. "I've been called a lot worse. He's a good kid. It was nice to get his emails every week." With a glance into the backseat, he checked on the sleeping boy. "How's he doing?"

Kristi hugged her giant bag to her chest and plastered on something that he assumed was supposed to resemble a smile. It came much closer to a grimace.

"He's...tired. All the time. He's not getting enough oxygen, and the doctor said that pretty soon he'll either have to carry around a canister or move into the hospital full-time."

That made sense. The kid's lips were borderline blue, and his breathing was too fast.

He shot another glance in Cody's direction.

But his gaze snagged on the *two* black vans that were now behind them. His pulse soared.

Snapping his focus back to the front, he saw what he'd missed before. A third van in the left lane, slowing down. In a few seconds it would be at their side.

The vans had set up a tactical maneuver.

He'd seen a thousand of them in training and in the field, and it didn't take him more than a second to work out what was happening. They were going to box him in. To what end, he couldn't be sure. Would they try to force his car off the bridge?

As if on cue, the van to the left jerked to a near stop, tires squealing and cars behind it laying on their horns.

The painful screech stopped Kristi's chatter. "What's going on?"

Zach motioned toward the van, then to the right, where another pulled up alongside them. They didn't seem to be trying to force him off the bridge, then— so what was their plan? He slowed way down, putting extra space between him and the vehicle ahead. It was a tractor trailer. Running into that could seriously injure him and Kristi and Cody. Was that the goal?

He continued slowing down to the annoyed honks of everyone behind them. But he didn't have another choice. There were three eastbound lanes and no way off the two-mile bridge. Traffic was hemmed in by a cement barrier blocking oncoming traffic on the left and a relatively low guardrail on the right. But with enough force, at the right angle, the car could go up and over.

And into the Pacific.

His stomach sank faster than a car in the ocean.

The van on the right was edging closer to them, while the one on their left held its position, keeping Zach from an evasive maneuver. Braking hard wasn't going to work either. Not with the third van right on their six.

Kristi gasped and covered her eyes, then nearly lunged for the backseat. "Cody."

Zach gave her a push until she was facing the front. "Sit down. Keep your belt on."

It was terse and a bit sharp. And all he could manage at the moment.

The van to the left pulled ahead while the one on the right veered into their lane. Zach didn't have another choice. He had to pull into the vacancy, even as the lumbering black beast on his right kept pressing them closer and closer to the divider. If they hit it just right, the front end could crumple in on them. Or they could flip over the divider into oncoming traffic.

He had to get out of there.

He had to get his family to safety.

Find the opening. Find the exit strategy.

His instructors had drilled it into him. There was always a way to escape. He just had to wait until it presented itself.

It took half a second to see it. He didn't pause to analyze. He just floored it. They shot ahead of the van on the right, which couldn't keep up with the lighter sedan. Zipping behind the semi and into the far lane, they shot forward into the clear. The vans tried to catch up, but the end of the bridge was in sight.

As soon as they were on land, he veered off to a side street, searching for a pursuit that didn't come.

Kristi's chest rose and fell rapidly, her panting breaths filling the otherwise silent car.

Zach narrowed his gaze and stared into her pinched features.

"You want to tell me what exactly I came home to?"

TWO

Zach eased Cody into the bottom bunk and pulled the covers under his chin. The little guy had slept through the whole ordeal on the bridge and even through the tense drive back to the town house. But now he let out a loud yawn, and his eyes blinked open.

"Is it nighttime?"

Zach leaned over Cody and shook his head. "Nope. But for now, you should get some rest. Have a good na—" he pulled himself up short "—sleep."

Cody yawned again and snuggled beneath the red blanket covered in classic Corvettes. "Okay."

Kristi watched everything from the doorway, and when he sneaked past her, she stayed put, her head never turning away from Cody's face. It glowed in two low beams, the headlights of a red '57 Chevy night-light.

After several long seconds, she followed Zach down the stairs toward the kitchen, tripping on his duffel, which he'd dropped by the front door.

This wasn't a good sign. He never left things lying around, but one quick trip up the stairs with the kid, and he'd already forgotten his usual routine.

"Sorry." He grabbed the bag and carried it through the kitchen before shoving it into the laundry room, which now housed a metal shelf between the washer and dryer and more types of laundry detergent than a grocery store aisle.

What else had she changed while he'd been gone?

But there were more pressing questions that needed to be answered first.

She worried her bottom lip between her teeth, her eyes unseeing. As if on autopilot, she grabbed a plastic cup, filled it with apple juice and held it out to him.

"I could go for a soda, actually."

"What?" She jumped at his voice and looked down at the cup in her hand, then back at his face. The blank mask she'd been wearing since the bridge fell away, and an actual smile dropped into place. "I'm sorry. I was thinking…"

"About who might have been trying to push us into the Pacific?"

Her brows locked together, fear flashing through her deep brown eyes, and he suddenly hated himself for being so blunt. But tiptoeing around an issue had never been his forte.

Looking away from her, he grabbed a can from the fridge and popped the top. Tipping it back, he took a swig. And nearly spit it out.

Diet.

Yuck.

Glancing over to see if she'd noticed his near spit take, he watched as she ran her hands over her hair, a wild mass of honey-colored curls that reached well past her shoulders and looked softer than satin. "I just don't understand," she said. "Why would someone do that? They were trying to…"

"Kill us. Yes." Her face paled, and he tried to keep his voice low and gentle. Not easy after a year with a bunch of guys who didn't do coddling. "And they wanted it to look like an accident."

She swallowed, the sound filling the otherwise silent kitchen. Pressing a palm to the counter and the other over her stomach, she took several great breaths as the fear in her eyes shifted into something that resembled anger. "My son was in that car."

The truth hit like a boot to the kidneys. If someone was after him or Kristi, Cody would have been collateral damage, and whoever was inside those vans didn't care.

If a six-year-old wasn't safe, none of them were.

Zach took a step toward her, and she matched it in reverse, keeping three feet between them. But she kept her chin up and her eyes open and said nothing.

"That was broad daylight, Kristi. Someone was blatantly targeting us."

"I know." Her words carried a subtle tremor that she must have noticed because she paused, straightened her shoulders and tried again. "They were after me."

His entire body went on high alert, every muscle tensing, every nerve crackling. She sounded so certain, but he needed more details. "Why do you think that?"

Neck and shoulders stiffer than a frozen tarp, she stared right into his eyes. "Because Jackson Cole pointed right at me and said he'd make me pay."

The floor seemed to disappear beneath him, and he stumbled to a stool at the counter. He pointed at the seat beside him. "Maybe you should start from the beginning."

She looked from the spot beside him to the juice in her hand several times before nodding, setting the cup in the sink and then padding around the end of the counter and swiveling onto the stool.

"I'm not even sure where the beginning is." She stared down at the granite counter.

"Why don't you try from the day I left?"

Another small nod. "I applied for a job right before you left."

"With the lawyers. Right. In one of Cody's emails, you said you got it. Are you still working there?" He'd told her she didn't have to work, but she'd insisted. She'd gotten to know one of Zach's neighbors—an elderly woman who lived alone—who was happy to keep an eye on Cody while she was at the office in exchange for Kristi driving her on a couple of errands every week. Kristi had told Zach that she needed to make friends and start a life here. So he hadn't argued the matter.

"I've been with Jessup, Jessup and Holcomb almost as long as you've been gone. I'm a part-time receptionist. Just fifteen hours a week. It's a prestigious firm with a good reputation—but the team isn't very big. The three partners, two junior lawyers and some paralegals and investigators."

"And you," he said.

"Yes, and me." Her voice petered out, and her gaze locked on something on the far wall. Something that hadn't been there a year ago.

It looked like a framed drawing, the reds and yellows of a crayon mostly inside the black lines of a muscle car. It must have been colored by Cody, who apparently loved cars. The ones he could stay awake to see anyway.

"So this Jackson Cole guy... He worked with you?"

"No." Her expression tightened. "He wanted Walt Jessup to defend him. He was—is—a well-connected, well-known drug dealer. And the city finally got the evidence they needed for a trial. Cole thought that Walt was the only one who could get him off the charges."

"But Walt refused?" It wasn't really a question. He'd put the pieces together easily enough.

"When Walt turned him down, Cole went nuts. He tore the waiting room apart, turning over chairs and breaking lamps." She pulled her hands into fists. Zach couldn't do anything but cup his hand over her arm as a silent reminder that she didn't have to carry the burden alone. "And just before he left, he pointed at Walt, then at me, and said he'd get even."

The fear in her voice twisted at his gut. He needed to fix this for her. Now. "When did that happen?"

"About four weeks ago." She looked into his eyes, hers steady. She was holding it together pretty well, all things considered.

But he didn't want her to hold it together. He wanted her happy and safe. And Cody healed.

"Is this the first time something like this has happened?"

She frowned. "The first actual attack. But I've seen them around. Not those vans exactly, but cars that I don't know parked on the street, watching us. And one night I came home and there was someone peeking into the windows. He took off before I could get a good look at him."

"Did you call the police?"

"Yes. Walt had called them after the waiting room incident. And I called the same detective. Sunny something…" Her voice trailed off, and he easily filled in the blanks.

"She took your statement, but you haven't heard back from her."

"Yes."

Zach let the story tumble over in his mind. Something didn't sit quite right with what she'd told him. Not that he didn't believe she was telling the truth. It just wasn't adding up to what he'd seen on the bridge—an organized attack.

Jackson Cole sounded like the type of guy who'd fly off the handle at any perceived slight. Not the type to plot and plan. It took patience and strategy to get three vans to run a specific car off the road. Men with those qualities didn't usually throw temper tantrums when they didn't get their way.

Besides, she still hadn't answered one key question. "Why you? There are at least a dozen people in the office. Why'd he pick you?"

"I'm not entirely sure. Maybe because I was the one who told him Walt wouldn't take a meeting with him. Or maybe because I was handy and he recognized my face."

Zach nodded but kept silent for a long moment. There had to be more to this situation. Had she been privy to some information that Cole needed to keep a secret? Had she seen something in a file she wasn't supposed to?

Maybe she didn't even know what she wasn't supposed to know.

But they'd figure it out. Together.

He slid his touch down the slender bones of her arm. At her hand, he pulled it into his, lacing their fingers and squeezing softly. Her hand fit so well into his grasp, petite and soft, just like the rest of her.

The urge to pull her into his arms nearly knocked him off his stool, but he wasn't free to do that. They had signed a paper in the judge's office that said they were man and wife. But that's all she'd agreed to. And he wouldn't push her for more. Not now.

Not ever.

Even if it nearly killed him.

He scrubbed his free hand down his face and looked away from her warm brown eyes.

He was all kinds of an idiot.

But he'd marry her again in a heartbeat if that's what it took to help Aaron's son. And he'd do anything to keep them both safe.

"First we have to call the police. Then I guess I'd better talk with Walt and see if he has any more information about Jackson Cole." Her eyes widened and Zach could see she wasn't pleased with the idea, but he had no intention of backing down. He was going to do whatever it took to protect her, whether she liked it or not.

This had been a terrible idea, but Kristi hadn't been able to talk Zach out of it. After a quick and unhelpful call to Detective Sunny Diaz, who'd said she couldn't help without license plates or models on the vans—neither of which they had—Zach had insisted they talk with Walt.

"It's okay," he said, his voice low as he stepped out of the car. He could probably feel the strain coming off her in waves.

He walked around the hood of the car, opened her door and held out his big, callused hand. The tips of his fingers were blunt, the skin toughened by hard work. Yet they were cupped in a gentle invitation.

Taking a deep breath, she put hers in his and let him pull her out.

"I don't want to lose this job. Do you know how hard it is to find a part-time job with flexible hours and decent pay? If Cody is having a bad day, Walt lets me make up the hours another time. And if I get a call from Mrs. Drummond that Cody isn't feeling well, I can leave at any time. I like working here, and they understand that Cody comes first. I don't think there's another job like this one."

Also, she hadn't told them that Zach was only sort of her spouse. They thought she was a military wife, and when they'd learned her husband was overseas they'd poured out to her. Bringing her food. Sharing a bonus check. Getting her car serviced. Offering her several extra days off when Zach returned.

But if they found out that they had a marriage built on necessity rather than love, would they feel like she'd taken advantage of their generosity?

Undoubtedly.

And she hadn't exactly told Zach that her boss thought they were really married either.

This could be a disaster.

His smile turned solemn, but the light in his eyes didn't disappear. "I won't put it in jeopardy." Taking a step closer and brushing an escaped curl behind her ear, he caught her gaze and held it. "You just have to remember that we're married. Everyone loves meeting a military man back from overseas finally getting to spend time with his wife."

"But where do I tell them you were?" She didn't even know the answer to that.

"I'll take care of it." Squeezing her hand, which he still held, he winked at her. "Promise."

Her stomach took a nosedive. They'd shared precisely twelve letters and four days together since they said their vows. But all the same, she trusted him. "All right." With a deep breath and a sigh, she followed him into the five-story office building. The only sound in the elevator was the light jazz that made his eyebrows go up, as though asking if it could be any more cliché. "We don't own the building. We just rent the top floor."

"Uh-huh. Sure." There was a subtle twinkle in his eye that said he was teasing her. And it was an unfamiliar sensation. She hadn't had inside jokes with anyone since Aaron, and it was a strange reminder of the little things she missed.

When the elevator doors dinged, she led the way and sent up a quick prayer that this wouldn't be awkward.

Lord, let us find some answers and let me keep my job.

As soon as they reached the lobby, the office seemed to erupt. At the front desk, Ginger popped up, her eyes bright and hands outstretched. "Are you Zach?" Her voice carried and heads popped out of open doors up and down the hallway.

With a glance toward the boardroom, Kristi let out a breath of relief that there was no meeting on the other side of the glass wall for them to interrupt. Turning back to Ginger, she opened her mouth to introduce him, but she was too late.

He gave a little bow and shook her hand. "Chief Petty Officer Zach McCloud. It's a pleasure to meet you, ma'am."

Ginger was barely thirty-five, only a few years older than Zach himself. She cooed at his formality. "Oh, Zach. Call me Ginger—everyone does. We've just been so eager to meet you. Where were you stationed?"

Of course. Of course, Ginger would start with the question that even Kristi couldn't answer.

But Zach's grin amped up, and he offered a wink, as though sharing a secret. "You wouldn't believe me if I told you. But I'm happy to be home." He snagged an arm around Kristi's waist. "With my family."

Ginger chuckled but didn't have time to respond as Teri and Trina, two blonde paralegals, descended on them. "Welcome home!" They spoke and moved as one, even though Teri was about eight inches taller than her counterpart.

Zach greeted them, too, all things friendly and jovial, but his arm never moved from around her middle. It was equal parts possessive and protective, and she let herself lean into his solid shoulder, trying not to analyze which part they were playing. Whatever he was doing was working. Everyone was at ease. Except for Kristi.

Then Walt arrived, his salt-and-pepper hair combed just right and a cautious smile in place. "Walt Jessup," he said, quickly shaking Zach's hand. "Thank you for your service."

"It's an honor, sir. Thank you for what you've done for Kristi."

"Oh, she's the one helping us. It's hard to find such a smart, motivated employee for a part-time position."

Her cheeks warmed at the praise. Clapping her hands over her face, she turned away. This wasn't going so badly—overly flattering compliments aside. Everyone was friendly and happy to meet him, and true to his word, he hadn't said anything worrisome.

Until he pulled Walt to the side. "I like the furniture in here. It looks new."

Her insides twisted into a knot. That was a blatant lead-in to the real questions he wanted to ask.

Walt laughed it off. "Oh, we had a little trouble in here a few weeks back. I'm sure Kristi told you. A would-be client trashed the whole room. But it was a good excuse to redecorate."

He nodded. "She did tell me. Have you had any more trouble with him?"

"I think he's long gone." Walt's poker face was too good for Kristi to be sure if he really had nothing more to share about Cole.

Before Zach could ask any follow-up questions, Trina shrieked, "You have to come to the Christmas party."

Zach rubbed the top of his head. "Christmas party?"

Walt slapped him on the back. "Of course. We have one for friends and family every year in the big conference room in the back. Food, dancing, plenty of holiday celebration. You'll come."

It wasn't a question, but Kristi still scrambled to find a reason to decline. "I'm not sure—"

"Sounds wonderful." Zach shot her a full grin and a knowing look that said he had a plan. Problem was, she had no clue what it was. "We'll be there."

THREE

Kristi rolled out of bed the next morning more exhausted than she'd been the night before. And no closer to coming up with a plausible reason why Zach shouldn't—couldn't—go to her office Christmas party. Nerves over the party mixed with fears over Jackson Cole, culminating in half-waking dreams where he appeared at the event. He'd screamed and pointed right at her in a way that was far too familiar for comfort, sending shivers racing down her spine.

She'd much rather stay under her warm blanket and pretend none of this was happening.

But the pitter-patter of little feet down the stairs reminded her that she had to get out of bed. Cody had a doctor's appointment that afternoon that he couldn't miss. No matter how much she wanted to hunker down inside and ride out whatever storm was coming for her.

The loud footfalls that followed the soft ones reminded her she didn't have to face it alone.

Somehow that was enough to get her out of bed and stumbling toward the kitchen. Pulling on her ratty robe, she nearly tripped over an uneven arm of the belt before catching herself on the wall with a loud thud.

"Everything okay up there?" Zach's voice was gravelly. Cody's sweet laughter quickly followed.

Grumbling, she straightened the belt and stomped down the stairs. When she reached the kitchen and the boys caught sight of her, Zach stopped his spoon halfway to his mouth, suspending an enormous bite of cereal and milk over his bowl. His eyebrows were at full mast, his mouth hanging open uselessly as he leaned against the counter beside Cody's stool.

"What?"

Cody giggled.

She swung her gaze on him, frown in place and eyes narrowed. "What's so funny?"

"It's—"

Zach dropped his soup spoon back into his bowl with a splash. "Nothing. Nothing is funny."

She caught her reflection in the stainless steel toaster on the counter. Her hair was a wild mass on top of her head, her curls stretching in every direction and dancing with every movement. She clamped her hands over her hair and tried to tame it.

It didn't help.

Neither did Zach's smirk as he picked his spoon back up and took a bite of his sugary breakfast.

She shot a glance in Cody's direction. He had a piece of whole wheat toast slathered in jelly sitting on a plate and a bowl in front of him. "Did you give him cereal? He can't have that much processed sugar."

"Relax, Momma."

She frowned at Cody's too-cool tone. Where'd he pick that up?

Cody tipped the bowl toward her. "Zach peeled me an orange."

"Oh." As comebacks went, it wasn't her best. But

she didn't have anything else to say. Except maybe that she'd overreacted. Maybe she was a little too on edge lately. Maybe sharing her house with a man again wasn't helping.

"I get it," Zach assured her. "He has to eat lots of fruits and veggies and lean proteins. And not a lot of all the other stuff."

She nodded slowly but couldn't help eyeing the brightly colored loops in his bowl.

He didn't seem to need a translator for her expression. "I know I have to eat the good stuff, too—and I usually do. But after a year without it, sometimes a man just needs his cereal."

"Yeah, Mom. Sometimes a man needs cereal."

That made her laugh out loud, and even Zach's eyes crinkled at the corners. Holding out his hand, he gave Cody a high five, which made Cody beam. It was clear her son had missed having a man around the house. It squeezed at her chest in a strange way, an odd reminder of grief and pride. She'd managed to keep going, to keep her family moving forward.

"So, I was thinking," Zach continued. "Christmas is only about three weeks away. And the living room is kind of bare. Maybe we should go pick out a tree this afternoon."

"We never get a live Christmas tree." Cody's tone pleaded with her.

"We used to. When you were younger. Before."

Zach met her gaze, and again he seemed to understand without more explanation. Aaron had handled the trees, until he hadn't. That first year after his death, she'd barely managed to get a three-foot tree up on an end table. But she'd done it for Cody. The next year she'd gotten a prelit tree from a box.

It wasn't the same.

She knew it. But it was the best she could do on her own.

But Zach had a way of reminding her that she wasn't on her own anymore.

"Anyway, we can't go today. You have a doctor's appointment this afternoon."

Cody immediately looked at Zach. "Want to go with us?"

"No, buddy." Kristi jumped in to save Zach from having to decline. He was just back from a year away. Certainly there were people he wanted to see and things he wanted to do. They couldn't assume his time was theirs. "I'm sure Zach has other plans today."

He slurped the last of his milk from his bowl and smacked his lips. "There's nothing I'd rather do than spend the day with you."

Cody held up his hand for another high five before shoving the rest of his toast in his mouth. "There's a car auction on TV." He hurried toward the living room, but his steps were sluggish, like he hadn't gotten ten hours of sleep the night before, even though he'd been asleep every time she checked on him.

Kristi watched him through the gap between the counter and cupboards, her heart breaking a little more, the way it did every day at the reminder of how frail her son was. She was so focused on him that she didn't realize Zach had moved to her side until he reached in front of her to pop his bowl into the dishwasher. His nearness made her jump.

"You don't have to go with us, you know."

His forehead wrinkled into three even lines as his lips pursed to the side. His eyes grew intense, but he kept his voice low. "We don't know when Cole might try again. But I promise I'm going to be with you when he does."

His words filled her with mixed emotions. He spoke like there was no doubt that Cole would try again, and the certainty raced through her veins like icicles in a Montana winter. But there was warm comfort in his promise to stay by her side.

Three hours later Zach was ready to go with them. He'd zipped up Cody's jacket, helped the boy into the backseat and climbed behind the wheel of the car before she'd even tamed her hair.

"Are you coming, Momma?" Cody yelled from his booster seat.

She slipped into the passenger side, buckling up before attempting to wrangle her hair into a ponytail.

Cody made a clucking sound. "I like it when your hair is down."

"Me, too."

She jumped at Zach's gravelly whisper.

The simple fact that he'd thought about the way she wore her hair made her fingers forget how to work. She lost her grip on the hair band, and it shot across the car, smacking into his shoulder. In a flash, he caught it and handed it back to her.

"I guess you don't agree."

"I didn't—that was an accident."

He shot a sly look in her direction. "Sure it was."

Those knowing looks he kept sending her way were making her stomach squirm. In an entirely not unpleasant way.

And she didn't like it one bit.

He was going to be close by until Cole was captured. She'd put up with it until then. And then she could put a little space between them.

Space. That's what she needed.

* * *

Zach followed Kristi's stiff directions to one of the hospital's side entrances. She hadn't said much since he'd teased her about her hair, and she'd leaned about as far away from him as she could get in the small car.

He made a mental note to keep his thoughts about her hair to himself. Which was too bad. She had gorgeous hair. Gorgeous everything, really.

But those curls. They were practically an invitation to run his fingers through them.

Not that he would. Ever.

At least not without a verbal invitation—which he doubted he'd ever get.

He found a parking spot and stepped out of the car. And just as he was about to open the back door, a white circle danced across the roof of the car. Like a reflection from a mirror, it bounced back and forth. But the angle was all wrong for it to come from another car.

He squinted into the sun, searching for anything that would cause it, but he couldn't see a thing.

As quickly as it had appeared, it vanished—leaving behind an unsettled feeling in his stomach.

"You okay?" Kristi asked. "Do you want me to get him?"

"No. I mean, I'm fine. I'll get Cody." He opened up the door, still looking over his shoulder, but there was nothing. No suspicious cars in the parking lot. No one on the roof of the adjacent building. Yet his senses were all screaming that something was about to happen. That he had to be alert.

As he set Cody on his feet and closed the door, he surveyed their surroundings one last time. The only other people in the parking lot were a family of four, including a baby in a car seat, and two nurses in their blue scrubs.

Maybe his body hadn't relaxed after a year of being on edge, every minute of every day. But this wasn't Lybania, and he wasn't facing terrorists. Maybe he was seeing something that wasn't there.

Except the shiver running down his back didn't ease.

Pressing a hand to Kristi's back and wrapping his other arm around Cody's shoulders, he ushered them toward the sliding glass doors that announced the cardiology unit. Cody shuffled his feet and nearly tripped over a low curb, but Zach grabbed the back of his shirt to keep him up.

"Want a lift, little man?"

Cody looked up with drooping eyes and a sad frown and gave him a quick nod.

He scooped Cody up in time to see Kristi mouth a quick "Thank you." Cody was small for his age but still too big for Kristi to carry very far. He couldn't help but wonder how she'd managed for so long on her own. Had she just powered through because there was nothing else to be done?

As they reached the sidewalk in front of the building, they moved to the side to allow a large group to exit. But just before they could step inside, the world exploded.

A gunshot split the crowd, its crack sharper than a whip. Every eye turned to the column right in front of Zach, a cloud of dust escaping from the fresh bullet hole. When a second shot rocketed past them, everyone screamed at once.

The noise was deafening. High-pitched and terrified, shrieks echoed off the side of the building, surrounding them and building fear with every reverberation.

He had to shut it out so he could do what needed to

be done. Protect the target. Identify the shooter. Those tasks were all that mattered.

Grabbing Kristi's arm, he spun them behind a large potted plant and squatted low. Running his hands up and down Cody's arms and legs in search of an injury, he demanded, "Were you hit?" When Kristi didn't answer, he jerked his head in her direction. "Were you hit?"

She frantically shook her head as another bullet tore through the shrubbery over their heads. He pulled her close, tucking her beneath his arm and covering her body with his, Cody sandwiched between them. He couldn't tell who was shaking—Cody, his mom or both. So he ran his hands up and down their arms to keep them engaged. He couldn't let them check out yet. Not when there was no telling what would come next.

What came next was more bullets in quick succession. He kept his breathing even and his hands steady. If only he could get a good look at the shooter. But when he tried to peek over the top of the large urn, another shot went off, this one far too close to his ear.

The others who had been by the entrance were long gone, sprinting toward their cars. Thankfully the sidewalks were clean. No sign of blood or injury.

Because the shooter was targeting only one person.

It made his chest ache and his head spin, and he couldn't hold Kristi's trembling form close enough. Her head fit under his chin, her shoulder beneath his.

"It's okay," he said. "It's going to be okay."

But his words didn't make the hail of bullets stop.

And then he heard the sweet song of police sirens. Just like that, as quickly as they'd started, the shots ended.

He didn't dare get up until every window and roof on the opposite building had been checked. Most likely the cops had scared the shooter off. But Zach wasn't about to play fast and loose with the lives in his arms.

He released Kristi just enough for her to look up at him, eyes wild and curls askew. Her face was filled with a hundred questions, but she only dropped her gaze to her son and cupped his cheeks in her palms. "Are you all right?"

Cody looked mildly shell-shocked but shrugged anyway. "I'm okay."

She turned her arm, and Zach saw a red swath from her elbow to her shoulder. Grabbing her with less finesse and more fear, he said, "I thought you said you weren't hit." The words were harsher than he'd intended, but the dread that clogged his throat demanded nothing less.

Kristi followed his gaze to the smear of blood and frowned, looking puzzled. "It's not me. I'm not…" Her eyes widened in alarm when she looked at his shoulder. "Oh, Zach."

She scrambled to pull off her sweater and pressed it against his arm.

Pain seared through him like a flash of lightning. It was as if his entire arm was on fire, and he hadn't even noticed. Only now could he feel the blood rolling down to his elbow.

But at least it was his and not hers.

FOUR

"I'm okay." As soon as he said the words, Zach knew they were a lie. Blood was still seeping from his arm, and his vision was already starting to go gray. If he didn't do something soon, he'd wind up flat on his back with a slew of doctors and nurses hovering over him.

He clamped his hand over Kristi's, pressing her sweater harder against his wound and squishing her slender fingers in the process. She didn't even flinch. Her eyes deep pools of concern, she leaned over Cody, closing the space between them.

"You're going to be all right. Help's on the way."

He pinched his eyes closed and nodded. "Swhat I said. I'm goo'." Was it just him, or did he sound like he'd gone a few too many rounds in a boxing ring?

Focus.

He had to stay alert. Stay in the moment. He had to keep them safe.

Kristi shifted her hand, her finger digging into his wound, and he nearly shot to his feet. He would have if her other hand hadn't cupped his cheek, her thumb taking a slow stroll along his cheekbone, sending his heart pounding.

No, that was the strain of the scenario. Had to be.

He leaned his uninjured shoulder into the cement planter and took a sharp breath. *Just focus on the pain. Don't think about silky hands. Or pretty brown eyes.*

Think about the shooter.

Vaguely he heard feet pounding toward them. Someone squawked into his radio. "Three civilians."

"He was hit!" Kristi cried.

Zach waved his hand to cut her off. There was no need for this kind of fuss. But before he could say anything, a tall black police officer squatted right beside them.

"How many times were you hit?"

"Once." Zach gave himself a moment to catch another breath and make sure he hadn't missed another injury. Legs? Fine. Abs? Okay. Chest? Still there. "Just my shoulder."

The officer nodded, repeating the news into his shoulder radio. When he turned to Cody, who still hovered beside his mom, the cop's voice turned gentler. "Were you hurt?"

The little boy shook his head before pointing. "Zach's bleeding."

"I know, and help is on the way."

The ringing in Zach's ears turned sharper, and he turned to lean his head against the planter, but Kristi caught him, cradling him against her shoulder and resting her cheek against the top of his head.

"How long does it take to get help? We're *at* the hospital."

The police officer seemed to understand that it was a rhetorical question. They were at the hospital—but at the cardiac unit. It would take a few minutes for the police to secure the area so the emergency responders knew it was safe to move in.

"Did you see the shooter?"

Kristi shook her head, her curls tickling the back of his neck. "I didn't see anything."

Zach tried to sit up a little straighter, but it turned into more of a slump. "He was on the building—" he flopped his good arm in the general direction "—across the parking lot."

Both the police officer and Kristi whipped their heads around as though they would catch a glimpse of the gunman.

The cop swung back just as quickly. "How do you know?"

"Saw his scope reflecting. On top of the car."

Shock crossed the cop's face. Zach guessed that most civilians didn't pay attention to strange reflections. Well, he wasn't a civilian.

"I'm a SEAL."

The surprise was replaced by something that could only be identified as respect. "I didn't realize."

Why should he have? Zach was out of uniform and out of sorts. On the ground and mentally fuzzy wasn't his usual stance.

But his family was safe. At least for the moment.

The cop turned his head and spoke into his radio, relaying Zach's information. "SWAT's going in to clear the area. It'll be just a few minutes."

"But he's been shot." Kristi's voice cracked under the strain. "Can't we get him inside?"

"Not without leaving him—and anyone helping him—exposed." The cop offered a half smile and tried for a little humor. "Besides, he's probably been hit before."

"Actually, no." Zach could remember a whole lot of

pain in his years with the teams, but this particular discomfort was new. Getting shot *hurt*. With a capital *H*.

The blood loss wasn't much better. It was making him woozy and far too focused on the gentle slope of the underside of Kristi's chin. The urge to touch her surged through him. He caught his hand at the last minute and forced it back to his shoulder.

Nope. He wasn't allowed to do that.

But she's your wife. Your very, very pretty wife.

Not exactly.

She signed the license.

But she hadn't agreed to anything more than a marriage in name only. Because she was scared and on her own and he'd offered to help. And he'd rather shoot his other arm than do anything to break her trust. Besides, he wasn't the kind of man she wanted. He never had been, and he didn't know how to be.

The cop's radio squawked, the words a jumbled mess, except for the crucial phrase "All clear."

In an instant, three nurses pushing a gurney charged into the open, their tennis shoes slapping against the cement and nearly covering the low squeak of one of the gurney wheels.

"Can you get up?" A formidable blonde leaned over him, looking like she'd pick him up herself if he wasn't able.

Everything in him wanted to stay where he was and fall into oblivion. But a stupid bullet in his arm wasn't going to keep him down. Not when the shooter was still at large, leaving his family in danger.

As he settled onto the gurney, Kristi grabbed his hand and squeezed it. "We're right behind you."

He closed his eyes and nodded but called out just before the nurses pushed him away. "Wait. I forgot…"

His voice trailed off, and he sucked in a quick breath, snatching at as much air as he could get before quickly releasing it, trying to remember what he'd forgotten. "Bad shot."

"What?" The cop stepped closer to him.

"The shooter. Had a scope but couldn't have been a pro. Was a bad shot."

Kristi shook her head frantically. "Bad? He *hit* you."

"But he was aiming for you."

Kristi couldn't stop pacing after the nurses wheeled Zach away. During the interview with the police officer, she covered a four-foot space innumerable times. While his cardiologist checked on Cody, she marched back and forth across the exam room. When Cody looked up at her with confusion in his wide eyes, she tried to stop. But the pull was too strong, and she took a quick side-to-side step.

"Mom?" Cody's voice was clear and strong, and she snapped to attention, noticing that the doctor had even halted his charting.

"Yes?"

"Are you all right?"

"Yes." Her second response sounded more like a question than the first, so she cleared her throat and tried again. "I'm fine. Everything's okay."

"No, it's not." Cody wasn't being disrespectful or snide. He was just stating the fact, and it tore at her chest. He was so innocent, and she wanted to keep him that way. But she couldn't deny that someone had shot Zach, or that that meant everything was very much not okay.

Combing his hair with her fingers, she tried for a

smile, but her mouth seemed to have forgotten how to shape it. "You're right, buddy. I'm scared."

He was aiming for you.

Zach's words rang in her head, terrifying and true.

"Not me."

Dr. Guthrie smiled as he pulled his stethoscope from around his neck. "You're pretty brave."

"Don't need to be." A smirk fell across Cody's face. "Zach promised he'd take care of us."

Zach.

He had the skills and training to protect them, and he cared about their safety. But even a SEAL could be brought down by a bullet.

Any man could be.

In an instant, she was back on the ranch while a uniformed officer, holding his hat in both hands, said, "I'm so sorry, ma'am."

"Sorry?" She nearly choked on the word.

Cops didn't come to your front door when the cows got loose. Still…she hoped. She prayed. "We've fixed that fence a half-dozen times. Silly cows. We'll get them rounded up."

"It's not your cows, ma'am."

Her mouth went dry, a fist in her chest twisting everything inside. She could only shake her head.

The cop's face crumpled. "It's Aaron."

She put up both hands as though she could stop him from breaking her heart. "Don't. Don't say it."

He didn't comply. "I'm sorry to have to tell you, he's been killed."

Ice covered her until she was too frozen to even shiver.

"He was shot at the gas station."

She hadn't even been able to cry. Instead, she'd sunk

to the floor and blacked out. The rest of that day had been a complete blank, not a single memory of her mother-in-law arriving and caring for Cody. Not the endless cups of tea pushed into her hands.

But when she staggered out from that stupor, her nightstand had been full of empty mugs, her bed turned into a cocoon of wool blankets.

She'd dressed in black and held Cody close as Aaron's casket was lowered into the ground.

It had been a fluke. People didn't just walk around and get shot. She understood that.

At least she thought she did.

But now her second husband had been shot, too. And men died from bullet wounds.

She wrapped her arms around her middle, trying to keep her mind from wandering down the hall to the ER, to where Zach was being treated for his wounds. The ER doctor had been very firm. She and Cody couldn't go with Zach while he had his procedure, so she might as well take Cody in to see his cardiologist while Zach was being taken care of.

Only she couldn't seem to focus on Dr. Guthrie's words as he jotted notes into Cody's chart.

"Mrs. McCloud?" The doctor sounded like he'd called her name several times, but she still jumped when his words broke through her consciousness.

"Yes? Yes."

Dr. Guthrie pointed at Cody. "How many hours a night is he sleeping?"

"About ten or eleven." She bit her lip, hoping that didn't mean more bad news. At his frown, she hesitated to add more, but it had to be said. "And napping three to four hours throughout the day."

He nodded, scribbled more and pinched his nose.

"Well, young man, your oxygen levels are getting lower, which is making you pretty sleepy."

Even now, Cody's eyes drooped, as if the effort of remaining upright on the exam table was just too much.

"What can we do?" She sounded defeated already. And she hated it.

Except...well, this was her son, her only child, her last connection to Aaron. She couldn't lose him. But as long as someone was trying to kill her, she would be distracted from Cody's needs, always wondering when Jackson Cole's lackey would pop up again.

It wasn't fair.

None of this was fair.

She grabbed for a tissue from the box sitting on the blue counter but had to physically restrain herself from picking up the whole box and chucking it at the wall.

Dabbing her eyes, she squared her shoulders and tried to keep her focus squarely on Cody's care. "What can we do?"

"I want you to talk with the transplant coordinator again. You know Denise Engle." It wasn't really a question, but Kristi nodded all the same. "Just make sure that you have everything in place if a match becomes available."

"Am I at the top of the list yet?" Cody asked. Kristi grabbed at his pointy shoulder to shush him. Cody sounded far too excited. Especially when she and the doctor both understood that his best day would be someone else's worst.

"I'm afraid not," Guthrie said. "But you're getting close. For now, you can stay at home, but..."

She knew that *but*. If Cody's condition continued to deteriorate, he'd need to be admitted until his transplant. Dr. Guthrie had warned her of that during their first appointment.

He'd have to leave his car models and his quiet room and his very cool night-light. And he'd probably miss most of the Christmas season.

Cody would hate it.

So she shook her head at the doctor. "Please. There must be something we can do."

He nodded slowly. "For now we're going to set you up with a portable oxygen tank." As he wrote a quick note on his prescription pad, he directed her to a medical supply store. "I want him to use this all day and at night." Turning his attention to Cody, he motioned long, narrow fingers toward his nose. "The oxygen will help you feel more awake, and it'll come through a tube that fits over your ears and right into your nose. Think you can keep it on all day?"

Cody shrugged. "I guess."

"You mean, 'Yes, sir,'" Kristi corrected.

Ducking his head in chagrin, Cody agreed. "Yes, sir."

Dr. Guthrie leaned in, a soft smile on his usually firm face. "If you have a hard time with it at first, take it out for five minutes every hour until you're used to it."

Suddenly Cody's face lit up, and Kristi had a feeling it had nothing to do with the doctor's five-minute reprieve.

"Zach!"

She spun so fast that her neck popped, but she hardly noticed when her gaze settled on the broad form leaning against the exam room doorjamb. His hazel eyes were bright and alert, and some of the color that had drained from his lips had returned. But his left arm was in a black sling, held tight against his body.

She sailed across the room, and before she could even process her own intent, she'd thrown her arms around his waist. It seemed to release a burst of a chuckle, which ended on a soft groan.

"Oh!" She jumped back in time to see him physically working to relax the lines around his mouth. "I'm sorry. Did I hurt you? What are you doing here? We were going to go to the ER right—" She waved toward the doctor. "We were going to go find you as soon as we were done."

He managed a strained smile. "No need. They patched me up and gave me some fluids and sent me on my way."

Dr. Guthrie eyed Zach with a heavy dollop of suspicion but said nothing. It didn't help the knot in her stomach. Zach swayed just a bit, and she almost grabbed for him before he leaned his good shoulder against the door frame.

His gaze never moved from hers, but there was a flickering in his eyes, a moment where he wasn't as focused as he wanted her to believe he was.

"I'm so sorry," she whispered.

"I'm not." Little lines took up residence around his eyes, even though the rest of his face didn't move. "Better me than you." His gaze traveled across the room. "Or Cody."

Her stomach churned. Cody had been only a few inches away from that bullet. She'd come far too close to losing the person she loved most in the world, and her only response was a three-word prayer. *Thank You, God.*

But what would happen if Cole found his mark the next time and Cody lost her?

FIVE

"Good morning."

Zach thought the greeting was innocuous enough, but Kristi still fumbled her coffee cup. He jumped out of the way just in time, letting the steaming joe slosh to the dark gray tile of the kitchen floor.

This wasn't the first time she'd dropped her coffee in his presence. Apparently he had quite the effect on her coffee-drinking habits.

But he couldn't be the only reason she was now trembling. Not after the shooting that had taken place just three days before.

"I'm sorry." Leaning her hand against the counter, she hung her head, presumably so she didn't have to look him in the eye.

"You thinking about Jackson Cole?"

This brought forth a Bambi stare—all big eyes and innocence—from beneath the fringe of her bangs. "All the time."

He moved to pat her shoulder, to offer whatever comfort he could, but stopped just short of her threadbare blue robe.

"Listen, we're going to get through this."

"How do you know? You don't know that! You don't

know what's going to happen. You can't control it. I mean—look at you."

True. His arm was in a sling, and his shoulder felt like it was on fire, especially after the pain medications from the ER had worn off. But he wasn't going to let that stop him from standing by her side.

From standing between her and Cole.

When the urge hit him again to reach for her, he didn't deny it. Running a hand down her arm, he squeezed her elbow. "We'll make it through together."

Suddenly she ripped her arm out of his grip, and the voice that emerged sounded wholly unlike her. Fire sizzled in her eyes. "Aaron used to say that."

His heart slammed against his breastbone at the agony in her words. He'd felt pain before at the loss of his best friend. But this was new. It wasn't the stinging reminder of Aaron and their summers running barefoot by the creek. It wasn't the missed stories they had yet to share or the shared past they'd rehashed a hundred times.

This was different. It wasn't his own grief that kicked him in the chest.

He ached for Kristi. His heart broke because hers did.

And he could offer only impotent promises about things he couldn't control. After all, she was right to remind him that he couldn't stop a bullet, that he couldn't control Cole, especially when he still hadn't been found. The cops had searched the hospital grounds, and the crime scene unit had hunted out any evidence. And they'd come up with nothing.

Which didn't make any sense. If the shooter was able to get away without leaving a trace, he had to know what he was doing. So how had he missed Kristi by almost two feet?

"We're—"

She whipped up her hand to cut him off. "Please. Don't."

"All right." He wasn't exactly sure what he was agreeing to, but it was certainly something she felt strongly about, so he was willing to comply. "What... what can I do?"

Her gaze swung toward the living room, where Cody's Corvette blanket hung over the arm of the couch, the little boy intent on a TV show about two guys who fixed up rusted-out muscle cars and resold them for more money than Zach earned in a year. The little man was either engrossed in it or he had sacked out for another nap.

"I'm scared." Her words were barely a breath, and he wasn't entirely sure she'd meant to speak them. Yet they tugged at the part of his heart that demanded he be honest with her.

"I am, too."

She spun to look into his face. "You are?"

"Of course. I got shot."

Just as he'd hoped she would, she let out a little laugh. Then she clamped a hand over her mouth as though she wasn't quite sure it was okay to laugh at his injury.

Better laughter than tears, he'd always thought. So he joined her.

"We're in the middle of something serious, and we have to find Jackson Cole before he strikes again." He shrugged his good shoulder, careful to keep the other unmoved. "As much as I hate to say it, I'm not at full capacity."

Her eyes narrowed. "How *are* you feeling? You've been putting on a brave face, but there was a lot of blood."

This was a little too much concern. Even from the woman wearing his ring. He wasn't completely unused to people caring about him—his brothers on the teams cared. They just showed it in a more…gritty way. So he blurted out the only thing that came to mind. "I'm sorry about your sweater."

"I don't care about the sweater. I care about—" Her jaw clamped closed, and she refused to continue.

But a seed of hope twisted its way inside him. Maybe she'd been about to say that she cared about *him*. He was almost sure of it. But he didn't like the way that thought made his heart kick a little harder.

He had to get them back on safer ground. "My headache is gone, and I'm not as tired as I was yesterday. Practically new."

She crossed her arms over her chest and frowned.

Okay, so that hadn't been enough to distract her.

"We've been holed up here for a few days. Maybe we could use some air." She didn't look convinced, but he pressed on. "Do you think Cody is up for a field trip?"

"Are you sure this is a good idea?" Kristi couldn't keep the hesitation out of her voice as she glanced over her shoulder at Zach, who was carrying a wide-eyed and excited Cody, who clutched the shoulder straps of the bag that held his brand new portable oxygen concentrator.

"Yep. Helping kids in need is always a good idea."

"Of course it is, but…" That's not what she had meant, and she had a hunch he knew it.

"Kids like me?" Cody pressed a hand to his chest, breathing deeply from the oxygen tube tucked into his nose.

Zach shook his head and pointed to the seven-foot-tall

Christmas tree covered in white paper angels at the end of the mall's open courtyard. Shoppers bustled between stores, barely conceding to the cool December weather with sweaters and long pants. Even Zach had only been convinced to put on a jacket because Cody had said he shouldn't have to wear one if Zach didn't.

"You see this angel?" Zach picked up one from the middle of the tree. Cody nodded.

"It represents a kid whose parents can't give him a present this year. This guy is six. Just like you."

Rubbing at his forehead, Cody frowned. "His mom can't get him even one?"

"None."

With a firm, decisive nod of his head, Cody said, "I could give him one of mine."

Zach chuckled, but a tear caught in the corner of Kristi's eye. Her son, who had so many struggles, who had already lost so much, was willing to give up his own happiness for another little boy he'd never met. When she sniffed at the unexpected emotions coursing through her, both of her guys looked at her like she had completely lost it.

Could they really blame her if she had? Her son needed a new heart. Her husband had just reentered their lives and added a presence—a *man's* presence—they hadn't had in more than two years. And Jackson Cole was trying to kill her.

If she wanted to cry because her son had the kindest little spirit, well…it was her party, as they said.

"What?" She might have sounded a little more confrontational than she'd intended, but she had no intention of backing down.

"Nothing." The corner of Zach's mouth quirked up

in a half smile. It was secret and soft and just for her. And it made her stomach do a strange flip-flop.

Oh, dear.

That was not good. Not good at all.

Turning back to Cody, Zach gave him a full smile and tipped his chin toward the volunteer standing next to the tree. "If we buy some presents for the guy on the angel card, she'll give them to him, and she'll tell him about how much Jesus loves him." Cody squinted, clearly deep in thought, as he scratched at the oxygen tube running across his cheek. "Do you think you could pick out a few things he might like?"

Cody nodded hard. "I bet he'd want some toy cars. And a toy tool set."

Zach looked thoughtful, his lips pinching to the side before he responded. "Excellent suggestions. Let's find them."

After signing up with the volunteer and promising to return with the gifts, Zach led the way toward a toy store. He never hesitated, pulling out his ID before the girl wearing the angel pin could even ask him for it, and then immediately turning in the right direction for the store.

"Have you done this before?"

He shrugged a shoulder. "Whenever I'm home over the holidays. It's my favorite thing to do at Christmas."

She bit back a laugh. "Shopping for six-year-olds?"

His gaze settled on her, warm and gentle like his touch. "I like helping people who need it."

Right. Of course.

People like the civilians he kept safe in foreign countries. People like the survivors he volunteered to help at the battered women's shelter here in San Diego that he'd told her about in one of his letters.

People like her and Cody.

Maybe they were just another charity case to him.

The idea twisted her stomach, oddly bitter.

So focused on her inner turmoil, she missed the rug on the floor and tripped over a turned-up corner. Catching herself on the strap of his sling, she squeaked and jumped back, managing to right herself. "Did I hurt you?"

Zach looked like it would take a tank to hurt him. His neck muscles flexed where they disappeared beneath the collar of his black jacket, and a tic in his jaw almost looked like he was holding back a smile.

But he only said, "I'll live."

"Okay. Good. Okay. Right." She couldn't possibly sound any more inane. But the sudden sense that she was being watched distracted her from the embarrassment. She whirled to see who was behind her.

There was no one there.

"You see something?" Zach whispered insistently into her ear, his lips practically brushing her hair. Which didn't do a thing to help the tremors in her hands.

"No. But…"

"Do we need to go?"

How should she know? She wasn't the trained warrior with half a dozen tours under his belt.

"Does it feel like there's someone watching you?" Zach pressed.

"I'm not sure." Her gaze roamed the crowded courtyard. There was no way to pinpoint a single face.

But Cole was tall—nearly six and a half feet. And the only man who towered above the crowds was a twenty-something surfer with a head of blond curls. Not the angry face and dark features of Jackson Cole.

"Then we'll go."

"No, but Cody."

Her son had already picked out a remote-control car, holding it up for them to see. "I bet he'll want this." But it was clearly an effort to hang on to the toy in question. He breathed quickly from the tube connected to the pack on his back.

She dropped to her knees in front of him, but Zach was there first, grabbing the toy car before it could hit the ground. "Can you breathe?" he asked.

"Uh-huh." Cody nodded, rubbing his forehead. "Just tired."

Now she didn't have to be a SEAL, just a mama bear, to know it was time to go. "Let's head home."

"But the car. He needs the car." Cody's voice rose, drawing the attention of the nearby shoppers.

"We'll get it later," she said, shushing him.

"What if we forget?" Cody shook his head.

"We won't forget," she said.

"But we might."

Why was he picking that minute to argue with her? She turned to Zach for support, but he had disappeared. Looking around the store, she spied him heading their way, a large white bag in hand. He held up his prize and shot her a coy grin.

"Got it. Let's go."

She didn't have time to ask him how he'd done that— how he'd circumvented a long checkout line and rescued them from a total Cody meltdown in front of all of those people. Maybe, like her, he'd sensed that Cody was wearing thin, so he'd taken action. He tended to do that. A lot.

"Want a ride, little man?" He barely waited for Cody's response before scooping him up and striding through the door.

Kristi had to almost run to keep up with him, and her feet kicked harder when she felt that tingle on the back of her neck again.

She wasn't imagining it. There was someone watching her.

When Zach whipped a look over his shoulder, she knew she wasn't the only one who felt it. He didn't say anything to her, but his gaze locked with hers, his eyes brimming with a harsh truth. They weren't safe.

"Stay close."

She nodded.

His voice went low as his gaze swept over the sheer number of people between them and the mall's entrance. "We're going to take a shortcut."

Before she could even register what he'd said, he veered into the crowd, bumping into a boy in a tank top and surf shorts. The kid groused. Zach never slowed. Kristi scurried to keep up.

Her heart was already pounding, her skin crawling. But she risked a glance behind her anyway.

A man in a dark jacket with a dark ball cap pulled low over his face made the same turn they had.

She wanted to lie to herself and say it might be only a coincidence.

It wasn't.

Zach grabbed her wrist. He pulled her close so that she fell into his back, but he never wavered. It took a moment to realize that he held her with his injured arm.

"Your sling—"

He cut off her argument with a single look, his eyes sharp and focused. Then he peered over her head, and she couldn't help but follow his movement.

The man behind them was closing in.

Zach's arm at her back tightened, and she spun in

time to see another man to their left, this one wearing big aviator sunglasses. As he hustled toward them, his jacket flapped open, giving everyone in the area a full view of the black handgun shoved into the waist of his jeans.

A girl screamed.

Kristi slapped her hand over her mouth, not entirely sure if the cry had been hers or someone else's. But there wasn't time to think about it. With a breath in her ear, Zach instructed, "Through that store. There's an exit in the back. Then left to the car." As he charged ahead, he squeezed again. "Don't stop for anything."

Glad for the reminder, she clutched his hand until her fingers ached. He didn't even flinch. Just flung open a glass door and led her through a maze of clothing racks.

The door closed and then swung open again. She didn't need the gust of cool air on her back to know that Baseball Cap or Sunglasses was right behind her. She prayed constantly in a two-word mantra. *Save us. Save us. Save us.*

Apparently God was listening because, despite the angry yelling of a store employee, they crashed through the back door into an empty loading area, no sign of either of their tails.

True to his plan, Zach made a hard turn, picking up speed and dragging her with him. Only then did she hear Cody laughing in Zach's other arm. "Faster!"

Zach obliged. Kristi rued every excuse she'd ever made for not going to the gym.

Zach seemed to know that she couldn't keep up. He glanced at her for a split second like he might just scoop her up and sling her over his shoulder. But then they reached the car. Zach ushered her into her seat, then whisked Cody into his booster before tearing out of the parking lot, breaking the posted speed limit that read 12 mph.

They zipped along, Zach checking his rearview mirror multiple times as they pulled onto the interstate.

Kristi could only dig her phone out of her purse and hold it up. "Do you want me to call the detective?"

Zach looked in the mirror again before shaking his head. "There's no rush. Not unless you recognized the guy in the hat."

"Why would I recognize him?"

He shot her a squinted gaze, his eyebrows pulled together to reveal two narrow grooves. "Not Jackson Cole, then?"

"Oh." It was all she could get out as she tried to make sense of the images racing through her mind. She hadn't expected to recognize him, so she hadn't looked closely. Besides, he'd had his hat pulled low. But she'd seen enough. "No. It wasn't him. Cole is a big guy. The guy behind us was too slim."

Zach nodded like he wasn't surprised.

"But what about the guy with the gun?"

Taking a deep breath through his nose, he squeezed the steering wheel until his shoulders flexed under the pressure. "He was a decoy. Someone to throw us off, but he wasn't a pro."

"How do you know?"

"A pro wouldn't have risked drawing the attention of the security guards by showing us his weapon. The pro knew better."

There was such certainty, such conviction in his words that she wanted to pull her knees up to her chin and hide until this whole situation was over.

But that wasn't an option.

Just as she took a fortifying breath, the phone in her

hand buzzed. She didn't recognize the number but answered it anyway. "Hello?"

"May I speak with Kristi McCloud?" The female voice was not at all menacing. Still Kristi hesitated before responding.

"Who's calling?"

"Detective Sunny Diaz with the San Diego Police Department."

"Oh!" Relief washed through her. "This is Kristi. I was going to call you."

"You were? Did something else happen?"

She quickly gave her the rundown of their ordeal at the mall, and she could hear the detective typing along to the rhythm of her words.

"Was there anything recognizable about them? Any noticeable birthmarks or tattoos?"

As Zach pulled onto the street in front of his town house, she shook her head. "No."

"There's not much we can do now. I'll check to see if there's any security camera footage, but if these guys were as cautious as you say, we probably won't find much."

She shouldn't be disappointed. She wasn't really. She hadn't expected anything else.

But there was a corner of her heart that had hoped.

"The reason I called—" right, Diaz had called her "—was to let you know that we found two burned-out black vans that match the description of the ones that tried to run you off the bridge."

"You found the vans?"

Zach parked, then leaned over as he unbuckled his seat belt. "Are there any prints? Any evidence?"

She repeated the question, and the detective's voice turned sour. "Not likely. They were pretty well destroyed in the fire, but we're searching both of them anyway."

"Only two?"

Zach's eyebrows lifted, and he held up three fingers. She nodded. She remembered.

"There were three vans."

"Huh. Well, no sign of the third yet. We'll keep an eye out, and I'll let you know if we find anything else."

"Thank you." She hung up and crawled out of the car, meeting Zach on the walkway to the house. As had become their norm, Cody was sacked out against Zach's shoulder.

"She said they didn't find a third van."

Rubbing his head with a flat palm, Zach scowled. "Why ditch two of them now? Especially if they're still coming after you."

"Thanks for the reminder." She tried to add a touch of humor, but her voice fell flat, weighed down with fear.

A frown settled across his features, and she couldn't look at him any longer. She reached for the door and grabbed the knob.

Suddenly his hand clamped over hers. "Stop!"

SIX

If Zach had had any hair on the back of his neck, it would have stood on end.

Kristi yanked her hand back, but he barely noticed as he swept the front door and surrounding shrubbery. Something was off. He knew it.

He just couldn't see it.

Handing off the boy in his arms, he said, "Take Cody and stand on the other side of the car."

For a split second it looked like she was going to argue. But there wasn't time for him to explain that something was off. That something had changed.

Instead, he cupped her cheek with his callused hand, her pale, smooth skin the opposite of his. "You'll be safer over there."

"Okay." With a nod, she carried Cody to the far side of her car.

Zach forced his attention back to the door, tiptoeing his fingers around the door frame. Nothing seemed out of place. Squatting low, he ran his hand along the weather stripping and under the metal lip of the frame. Nothing.

He narrowed his gaze and pressed his hand flat against the door. It wasn't warm to the touch and didn't open.

Maybe he was being overly cautious.

Hanging his head and scratching at the back of his neck, he closed his eyes to picture the house as it had been two hours before. It looked just like it always did. Black door against white siding. A brick facade on the double garage. Three green bushes lined up in the mulch along the front of the house.

He couldn't think of any discrepancies. Maybe it was his flagging adrenaline following the chase or an overactive imagination. Maybe...

No. Something had triggered his protective instincts.

He shot a quick look at Kristi, who stood right where he'd told her to. Cody stood beside her, awake now and leaning into her hip.

"Stay put. I'm going inside."

Kristi nodded.

Right as his hand reached the knob, he jumped.

A large oil smudge hooked over the side of the silver knob.

It hadn't been there when he'd pulled the door closed behind them on their way to the mall. Even if he hadn't seen it, he'd have felt it as he twisted the handle.

Someone had been here. While they'd been running from at least two thugs, someone had been at his home.

Whether they'd made it inside was another question.

His heart stuttered once —a telltale sign that he was geared up for whatever was inside these doors. He reached for his weapon, but his hand came up empty. He was supposed to be on leave—he'd left it in his gun safe.

Nice work, Einstein.

Grumbling at his stupidity, he unlocked the door and opened it a crack. It groaned, but no more than usual.

Sunlight flooded through the open blinds in the living room, catching nothing out of place.

He swept the kitchen and laundry rooms in one motion before hustling up the stairs. First, his—no, *Kristi's*—room. He rifled through the closet. Empty. Then the master bath, which smelled of flowers. It had never smelled like that—not even close—when this was his bathroom. But what would it be like…

His gut took a sharp jab, and he squared his shoulders against the reminder that he would never get to share this space with the woman who made it so sweet. That wasn't their arrangement. He'd promised to care for her. To honor her. To protect her.

But love wasn't on the table.

If she fell in love again, it would be with a stable guy. She'd chosen Aaron for a reason. Steady, established, available. It's what she'd always wanted, always needed.

And it wasn't Zach. He went where and when the teams needed him. Sometimes with no warning.

He was asking for a world of hurt if he let himself fall down the trap of dreaming of a different ending with Kristi this time. She'd made the right choice at sixteen. She wouldn't make a different choice at twenty-seven.

Refocusing on his search, he whipped through Cody's room and finally into his own.

Empty all.

Maybe their visitor hadn't made it inside.

The knot in his stomach suggested *maybe* wasn't good enough where Kristi and Cody were concerned.

Reaching into his closet, he opened the safe, pulled out his handgun, double-checked the safety and tucked it into the back of his waistband beneath his jacket.

By the time he poked his head out the front door, his heart rate had returned to a steadier pace. Still slightly elevated, but not the rushing he'd known when he'd first stepped inside.

Kristi and Cody hadn't moved. He hustled to them and scooped Cody up. "How about we make dinner?"

Kristi frowned, and Cody sighed. He drooped in Zach's arms, the rhythmic chugging of his oxygen pack their constant companion. But it wasn't enough. Cody was fading.

"Maybe a nap and then dinner," Zach amended. Cody didn't seem to have the energy to argue, so he hurried them back inside. While he tucked the little guy into his bed, Kristi clanked a few pots together in the kitchen. And by the time he made it back down the stairs, she was pouring rice over a bed of chicken in a glass pan.

She didn't even bother looking up before she spoke. "What happened earlier?"

The words choked in the back of his throat, and he weighed which ones he should say aloud. "I'm not sure." He considered a few possible explanations and settled on the gentlest truth he could find. "Someone was here."

She froze like she knew what he wasn't saying, and it made his chest squeeze. He fisted his hands beneath his arms to keep from pulling her close and promising her things he couldn't deliver.

"Here?" She dragged out the word. "You mean, inside the house."

It wasn't a question. Either he hadn't chosen his words very carefully, or she was learning to read him. Even without looking in his direction.

And he wished she would. Look at him, that is. He had a hunch that seeing her big brown eyes might make what he had to say a little easier. But she didn't. Instead, she pulled a tube of aluminum foil out of a drawer.

Funny. He hadn't kept aluminum foil there before

they moved in. She was rearranging more than his schedule.

"Yes. Probably."

"How do you know?" She was so matter-of-fact about it. Her words were even and unaffected. Only the twitch in her cheek told him that she wasn't as calm as she was pretending.

Somehow that made the band around his lungs loosen. At least if she was scared, she'd be cautious. Vigilant.

"A smudge on the door handle."

Both of her eyebrows rose like she was going to need more than that.

"It was about the size of a finger, but there was no fingerprint. I'm betting someone wearing gloves closed the door last."

"What did he do?"

He pinched the bridge of his nose and hung his head. "Nothing that I can see."

Kristi frowned as she finished covering the casserole. "What's the point of breaking in, then? And if the bad guys were looking for us here, who was chasing us at the mall?"

"Good questions." Just not ones he had answers for. He could conjure up plenty of scenarios where one bad guy kept an eye on them, but why would another one come to the house but not leave a trap?

Easy.

He wouldn't.

A cord in his stomach began twisting, winding tighter with each breath.

Cole wasn't an idiot. He knew where they lived. He'd tracked Kristi down at least three times. And he wasn't working alone.

"We know Jackson Cole has at least two other guys working with him, or they couldn't have pulled off that stunt on the bridge." He scrubbed at his face, needing to say the words out loud. "And just orchestrating something like that takes guts and planning. He's a smart guy. He had a chance to plant some sort of trap for us while we were away from home. Why not take it?"

"I don't know." Kristi shook her head as she picked up the pan. "Open that for me?"

Zach grabbed the oven handle, his gaze following his hands.

Suddenly the overhead light glinted off a thin wire wrapped around the oven door.

His heart stopped.

Apparently question asked and answered. Cole *hadn't* missed this opportunity.

He ran his finger along the wire, following it until it disappeared above the hinge on the lower cabinet door. Pressing his hand against the dark-stained wood, he took a deep breath, trying to slow the wild gallop of his pulse.

He already knew what he was going to find on the other side. But he pulled it open anyway.

"What are you doing?"

With a quick glance over his shoulder, he squinted at Kristi, who was looking at him like he'd lost his mind.

"You might want to set the chicken on the counter and step into the hall."

"What? Why? It's ready to cook."

Zach slipped open the cupboard door only far enough to catch a glimpse of the brown cardboard box inside with the wire running right into it.

Yep. There was a bomb in his kitchen, and it had

been rigged to go off when someone opened the oven. When *Kristi* opened the oven.

Tongue dry and face numb, he closed the cabinet door, the hinge squeaking painfully, and Kristi jumped, nearly dropping the chicken. But she didn't set it down.

"What's in the cupboard?" she demanded.

This was not the time to mince words, so he dropped it as succinctly as possible. "A bomb."

Her face didn't move, except for a little twitch in the corner of her eye, which was followed by the rapid rise and fall of her chest.

Grabbing for her shoulder, he offered a gentle squeeze and whatever comfort he could.

Before he could even release his grip, she blinked, straightened her shoulders, put down the casserole dish and locked her gaze with his. "What do you want me to do?"

"Get Cody. I'll meet you at the front door."

She nodded, already at the kitchen's open entrance. "What are *you* going to do?"

"I'm going to get some backup."

There was no one he'd rather have in a situation like this than one of his SEAL brothers. But half of the team had turned into family men, and despite the danger they faced on every mission, Zach wasn't going to invite them to find more of it in his home. Will had just told them that he was going to be a dad.

The married guys were out, which left Jordan.

Jordan would rip him up one side and down the other—in the most brotherly of ways—if he didn't call him in for this.

Plus, Jordan lived about a mile and a half down the road. He'd probably beat the cops by five to seven minutes.

He snagged his phone out of his pocket and tapped

Jordan's number. The last number he'd called—besides Kristi.

"Hey, man. How's the shoulder?" The words seemed to dance through the phone, Jordan's amusement on clear display.

"Fine. Listen. There's a situation."

"Like you've developed gangrene or a situation like you finally kissed your pretty wife?"

Zach nearly dropped his phone.

This was the worst possible time for him to be thinking about kissing Kristi. Not that he hadn't before. Once or twice. Or a dozen times since he'd come home.

But he needed to focus on the bomb in his kitchen. Not the pretty woman sharing his house, filling his life and wearing his ring.

God, I need help. I have to get my head on straight.

"More like there's a bomb in my house. And I'm about to disarm it."

"More like?" Jordan sighed. "Or exactly like?"

"The second one." Zach closed one eye and stared at the ceiling with the other. "Can you bring your flak jacket?"

"Aw, man! I just got a new truck." Jordan's laugh was free of any humor. "I'm parking two blocks away."

Zach nodded. "Hope your new truck can move as fast as your mouth."

Jordan mumbled something completely unintelligible, then ended the call. Zach turned toward Kristi, who had disappeared and reappeared with Cody within a matter of minutes. Her eyes were filled with fear, and she'd clamped her teeth into her lower lip, but she was still and silent, holding it together like a seasoned pro.

"What will you do when backup gets here?" she asked as he ushered them out the door.

"Disarm it."

"Is that safe? Shouldn't you wait for the police?"

He shrugged. "It's hardly my first rodeo. I'm not the expert on the team—that would be Matt Waterstone. But I can't call him in. He's got kids."

Her gaze darted to Cody, questions filling her eyes. "Is he…?" Her question trailed off, but he had no trouble filling in the holes. Yes, Cody was in danger. They all were. His only answer was a slow nod.

She bit even harder into her lip, but it couldn't stop the low tremble there and it hit him like a sucker punch to the kidney.

"But I've got help on the way. Jordan will be here in a minute and then—"

"You rang?" Jordan jogged up to them and tossed a black vest at Zach.

He grabbed it out of the air as Cody craned his neck to get a good look at the new arrival. He couldn't blame the kid. Jordan was a sight the first, second and twelfth time you saw him. Built like a house, broad and thick and laced with steel. He didn't know how to back down— which had saved Zach on more than one occasion—and he never crumbled.

"Jordan Somerton." He shoved his hand out first to Cody, who shook it fast, then to Kristi, who offered him a wavering smile. "You must be Kristi and Cody." Hitching a thumb in Zach's direction, he said, "This guy showed your pictures to everyone who'd stand still long enough while we were deployed."

"You're a—a SEAL, too?"

"Yes, ma'am." Jordan pressed his baseball glove of a hand to his forehead in a mock salute. "Now, where's this surprise you promised me?"

Zach nodded toward the house to indicate their

bomb, but then reconsidered Kristi and Cody. He couldn't leave them outside and unprotected while he and Jordan got to work. "Can they wait in your truck?"

Kristi shook her head. "We're fine out here."

Jordan flipped her his keys, which she caught in a two-handed, unsteady grip. "Bring it back with a full tank. It's the white truck about a block down the road."

She looked about ready to argue, so Zach caught her eye. "Please. For my peace of mind. Call the detective, let her know that I'm inside—I don't want to get shot again." He offered a dry chuckle, but only Jordan gave him a half-grinned response. "They should send the crime scene unit. Then lay low until they get here."

After a long pause, she nodded, scooped up Cody's dragging blanket and scurried toward the truck.

The knot that had been slowly building inside him released its tension by half, and he sucked in a full breath, his first since he'd seen the wire. "Let's get this thing done."

As Jordan trotted behind him into the house, the two men donned their vests. They flipped open the cupboard door, clipped the trigger wire and analyzed the bomb on the bottom shelf. Jordan let out a tense hiss of air through his teeth. "This wouldn't have just blown the cupboard and the stove."

Zach nodded. "It would have ignited the gas line and lit up the whole house."

"Uh-huh." Jordan pulled a pair of needle-nose pliers out of his pocket and poked at what appeared to be a loose wire. It pulled taut, and he sucked in a harsh breath. Zach's heart slammed into his throat as he realized they were looking at a fail-safe.

Jordan rummaged through the wires, his fingers sure

and steady, as Zach peered over his shoulder, holding a flashlight beam on the right spot.

"This guy knew what he was doing. He's good."

Jordan snipped another wire and pulled the box free, so they could see it in the clear.

It was neat, tidy and deadly.

Zach couldn't shake the seasick feeling in his stomach. "If he's so good, why'd he miss a shot at Kristi by almost two feet at three hundred yards?"

Jordan shrugged. "Maybe he's a bad shot."

Narrowing his eyes, Zach shook his head. "The guy who made this—who put in the time and had the know-how to get this so precise—would he really have fired a weapon from across the hospital parking lot if he's a bad shot?"

"This guy?" Jordan's deep brown gaze swooped over the hand-sized explosive that had nearly taken out Zach's whole family. Every wire had a place, every corner bent to precisely a ninety-degree angle. "No. Whoever made this wouldn't miss his mark."

That's what Zach was afraid of.

SEVEN

Kristi spent the entire night kicking her blankets off and then pulling them back on. She flopped on one side, then flipped to the other. Nothing felt right. Nothing was comfortable.

Especially not the brief exchange she'd overheard between Zach and Jordan hours before.

As the cops had disappeared with the remains of the bomb, Jordan bid his farewell, too. After giving Cody a fist bump and telling him to take care of Zach, he turned to Kristi and tipped his head with a mock salute. "Pleasure to meet you, ma'am. Hope to see you again soon." He left unspoken the hope that it would be under better circumstances next time.

Zach walked Jordan toward his car, and as she steered Cody in the direction of his bedroom, she heard something she was sure Zach hadn't meant for her to.

"Call me if this happens again," Jordan said, his voice deep and a little gravelly.

Zach nodded. "I will. But I hope I don't need to."

Kristi pressed herself against the hallway wall as Cody reached the top of the stairs and Jordan's voice dropped. "He didn't get what he wanted."

"I know." Zach sighed, and she could picture him

rubbing the top of his head in the way he did when he was thinking through what he was trying to say. "But it just doesn't make any sense."

"What's that?"

"How could he miss?"

There was a long silence, and she imagined the two men—nearly equal in height and breadth—staring eye-to-eye.

She didn't know what the bomber missed, but she couldn't move as she waited for them to say more.

"Like I said before. This guy wouldn't miss. Not by two feet. Not from that parking garage."

Her chest seized to a halt. They were talking about the shooting at the hospital. Because, of course, they were connected. Of course, the man who left the bomb was the same one who had shot at her.

But why was Jordan saying that the shooter wouldn't miss? Of course, he'd missed. Unless...

Her mind tumbled the scenarios around and around, every one making her stomach ache a little more.

Unless the shooter had been aiming for Zach. After all, Jackson Cole hadn't said he'd kill her—he'd said he'd make her pay. And what better way to cause her pain than to make her lose a husband all over again?

Zach had grumbled again. "I know. That's why I'm worried."

If he had been worried, then she needed to be, too.

After flipping her covers off, she marched to the bathroom, splashed some water on her face and pulled on her robe. Yanking on the knot at her waist, she gave herself a decided nod in the mirror, ignoring the way her morning hair flipped out like a pop icon's from the seventies.

She wasn't going to wait around for Cole to find her.

Not when he seemed to have inside information about her every move. How did he know so much about her and her daily activities?

She had no clue. But she had an idea where they could start.

Kristi made it halfway down the stairs to tell Zach about her plan before she heard a cheerful ruckus coming from the living room. Someone had put Christmas carols on the radio, and Cody was singing along—off-key and about two beats behind.

She swung into the room to find Cody lying on the floor, gluing neon puffs on a red-and-white stocking. He looked up, his gap-toothed grin too wide for her to ignore.

Pointing to his art project, Cody laughed. "I'm making one for Zach. For Christmas Eve."

Her attempt to return his smile was a complete failure, and she wrapped her arms around her middle to keep herself from flying apart as her gaze swept over the rest of the scene.

The "Jingle Bells" music wasn't coming from the radio. Zach, sitting at the upright piano, which she'd assumed was purely decorative, pounded away on the keys. His grin matched Cody's in enthusiasm and joy, but his tone was perfect. She'd never heard him sing before, but he had a pleasant voice, low and soothing.

The whole scene was picture-perfect. But it wasn't supposed to be *him* in the picture. This was wrong. It was all wrong.

Her eyes filled with tears before she could even begin to identify why. There weren't words for whatever this emotion was that filled her chest and pressed on her heart until it felt like it might pop. There were only tears. And then a sudden outburst.

"Stop it. Just stop it."

Cody looked up with startled, unblinking eyes as the piano music slammed to a stop.

She risked a look in Zach's direction, expecting warranted censure. Instead, his face was calm. His eyes were filled with a mix of questions she couldn't answer and tenderness she didn't deserve.

She scrambled for something to say to fill the awkward silence. "Just don't…don't work on that now. It's too early. We're going to hang stockings on Christmas Eve. Like we do with your—"

Father.

Except Aaron was gone. This was their third Christmas without him. So why did it feel like the first all of a sudden?

Tears streamed down her cheeks, and she spun, rushing for the safety of her room.

Behind her, Zach spoke to Cody, his words hushed and soothing. "Sit tight, little man. I'll be right back."

Kristi slammed her bedroom door and fell back against it. No matter how hard she tried to catch her breath, it was always an inch away.

Suddenly the door at her back rattled, the knock soft and words softer.

"Kristi? Are you okay? Do you want to talk about it?"

No. She most definitely did not want to talk about it.

Apparently Zach couldn't read her mind. "Talk to me. What was that all about?" The door rattled as he leaned against it. "Please let me help."

How could he help when she didn't even know what was going on in her own mind?

She choked back a sob that wanted to escape and forced out, "I'm okay."

He didn't respond for a long moment, the quiet hanging heavy between them. Screwing the heels of her palms into her eyes, she tried to shut off the waterworks, which just gushed harder.

"I'm sorry."

Why was he apologizing? He wasn't the one who'd flipped out over an off-key Christmas song and a badly decorated stocking.

Zach cleared his throat but kept his voice whisper low. "I forget sometimes. You're so capable and confident, and I forget that this is all new to you. I'm trained to handle this kind of stress. But this isn't your norm. And it's not an easy situation."

She turned and rested her forehead against the door. "Why are you being so nice to me?" From Montana to the present, there was no explanation for him disrupting his whole life for her and Cody. And now it seemed as if his very life was in danger because of her. Why would anyone risk that?

Except maybe he was just that good of a man.

"You've had a hard week—a hard couple years. Nobody blames you."

With a little snick of the door, she opened it far enough to catch his gaze, which was filled with warmth. The little cleft in his chin popped as he offered her a half smile.

"I feel like such an idiot."

"You're not." His tone left no room for argument, but it didn't stop her from trying.

"I yelled at my son because decorating stockings and singing Christmas songs was something we did with Aaron." Gathering a full breath, she let out the truth in a rush. "And it hit me that it's never going to be like that again."

A muscle in his well-defined jaw jumped. Then he held out his hand, an unmistakable invitation. When she slid her hand into his, warmth seeped through her veins until it swirled through her chest, thawing the fear that had frozen there. He gave a gentle tug, and before she realized what had happened, she was surrounded by him. His arms around her back held her close as she rested her forehead against his chest.

"It's been more than two years. I'm supposed to have moved on."

"Who told you that?" He didn't wait for her response. "Whoever said that is a liar. There is no *moving on* when you lose someone you love. It just gets a little easier. To breathe. To move. To live."

"But it's not easy," she argued. "It's still so hard. I'm worried about Cody and his heart. He's going downhill. I didn't sleep at all last night. I was replaying yesterday over and over. What if that bomb had gone off? What if you hadn't seen it? Or hadn't been here? I don't think I can wait for the next attempt. The police are only hitting dead ends. I have to do something to find Cole, but I feel like he's always ahead of us. How does he know where we are all the time?"

"I've been wondering the same thing." His chest rumbled below her ear.

Her arms squeezed his waist a little tighter. "Do you think maybe—could someone at my office be feeding him information?" His whole frame tensed, but he didn't speak. "Like which days I'm working and when I'm not. Walt always has a schedule of Cody's doctor's appointments, so he knows when I'm unavailable."

"You think someone you work with would be willing to share information like that?"

"I don't know." She sighed hard. "Maybe if they were

tricked or threatened. But the reasons for it aren't important right now. I just know that Cole seems to have that information—and I have to do something."

"I've been thinking about that, too. Well, not that you should do something. Me. I have to find him before he finds us again, and I have an idea."

"Me, too." But he might not like hers very much. "You go first."

"You said that Cole is involved in drugs. My friend Amy Delgado is a DEA agent—he might be on their radar. I'll call her this morning and see if they have any leads for us."

"Good. That's a good idea."

"And what's your plan?"

She tried to relax in his arms, but something about confessing her idea—and being this close to him—had her body curling in on itself.

"That bad, huh?" A note of humor tinkled through his words as his arms flexed.

"Somewhere in my office there's a file on Cole. If I could find it…"

His embrace turned more steel than shifting sand. "Why don't you just ask for it?"

"And risk alerting someone there that I'm looking into Cole? If someone is feeding Cole information about my schedule, who knows how deep they are in with him."

"But why not ask Walt? He was threatened, too, right?"

She nodded, hating the direction of her thoughts, hating more that they might be accurate. "Yes, but he hasn't been harassed at all. What if he's the one working with Cole?" She didn't want to believe it of her kind, loyal boss. She didn't want to believe it of anyone at the office. But she didn't know whom she could trust.

He hooked a finger under her chin and lifted her face toward him. But she couldn't meet his gaze. She refused to analyze whether it was because she didn't want him to read the fear in her eyes or because his touch on her face was making her insides a little too jiggly.

"I can get in and out during the holiday party tonight. No one will notice."

He chewed on the corner of his mouth for a long second but finally nodded. "Okay. If the DEA can't help us out, we'll go."

"Wait. We? No." She grabbed for a steadying breath as she pushed away from him. Space. She needed a little space to think.

But he interrupted. "Yes, *we*. Cole has been one step ahead of us everywhere we go, like you said. And if there's really someone in your office—someone who will be at the party—under his influence, no way am I letting you go in there alone. Period." He cringed, like maybe he hadn't meant to sound so much like a caveman.

"But what about Cody? We can't leave him alone, and we can't take him with us." There. That would put a pin in his argument.

"I'll call Luke and Mandy." Or not.

Zach had mentioned Mandy before. But just because she was a friend of his didn't mean Kristi was ready to trust her with Cody.

She must have projected her hesitations across her face because he swooped in. "Mandy is a physical therapist, and Luke is a navy medic. They can handle anything that comes up. We'll only be gone for a couple hours."

"I can go alone to the party. I'll slip in and out and be back in forty-five minutes."

He put his hands on his trim hips and shook his head. "You're not going alone."

Her mind warred at his words. Part of her wanted to yell at him that she'd been doing just fine on her own for the last two years and she didn't need his help. But the other part of her screamed that this was new and terrifying, and she couldn't control this situation any more than she'd been able to control Aaron's death. And if anything happened to her, Cody would have to deal with losing a parent all over again.

She couldn't even stomach the thought of putting her brave little man through that.

Swallowing her initial reaction, she nodded once. "Fine."

Zach visibly relaxed. "And first I'm calling Amy."

Zach held his breath as the phone on the other end of the line rang. He needed Amy Delgado to pick up. He needed answers. And he needed them quickly. He couldn't protect Kristi and Cody without a little intel. That's where interdepartmental relationships came in handy.

"Delgado."

"Amy. It's Zach. McCloud."

"Uh-huh." Rats. She didn't sound particularly happy to hear from him. Probably because the last time they'd talked, he'd had to call her to tell her that Jordan had to cancel their first—and only—date.

It wasn't his buddy's fault, though. Jordan's sniper skills had been required on a special operation, and he hadn't had time to call her himself before he went wheels up. And he sure hadn't been able to talk about the very classified mission after the fact.

As a result, Amy hadn't warmed back up to Jordan after the broken date and perceived slight.

Maybe she hadn't warmed back up to Zach either.

"What do you want, McCloud?" Her words were clipped but not entirely unkind.

He moved forward like walking on ice. "I got married last year."

"I heard."

Right, because she was still friends with another one of their SEAL team members, Will Gumble, whom she'd helped get planted in a Panamanian drug cartel in order to rescue his now wife.

"My wife is in trouble."

Amy must have been at her computer; the keys on her keyboard clacked at a steady rhythm. "Uh-huh."

"She had a run-in with Jackson Cole."

The typing stopped, and she sucked in a sharp breath. That…really wasn't the reaction he'd wanted. He'd been hoping she'd ask, "Who?" which would mean this guy wasn't as dangerous as he and Kristi feared.

Instead, she said, "What happened?"

He spelled out the event at Kristi's office. "And someone's been targeting her."

"Targeting how?"

"He took a few shots at her."

"I heard you got hit."

Was there anything this woman hadn't heard? Except the truth about why Jordan canceled their date, of course.

"And a bomb at our house."

She hummed low in her throat. "A bomb? That's

pretty out of character for Cole. He's a traditionalist. Guns and drive-bys."

So he wasn't afraid to get violent, but he liked to keep his distance. And maybe he wasn't too worried about precision. Hence Zach's shoulder. But that didn't mesh with yesterday's setup. "Any chance he's working with someone who's into bombs?"

"I don't know. He hasn't been on my list in a while. But let me ask around. Someone else may be keeping tabs on him, especially if he has a hit out on a civilian." She paused for a long second. "Listen, I'm sorry this is happening to you guys. You don't deserve this."

"And I'm sorry about…" He bit his tongue, wishing he hadn't gone down that particular path. But it was too late now. "Well, about that thing with Jordan."

"Sure." He could hear the stiffness in her voice. Despite the benign word, her tone had zero give. "I'll call you if I hear anything about Cole."

"Appreciate it."

He ended the call and stared at his phone before scrubbing his hand across his face. Amy was barely an ally thanks to Jordan's less-than-smooth moves, but she would help out if she could. He was sure of it. She was a good woman, a good agent. And he'd heard the sympathy in her voice.

But so far she'd managed to confirm only one thing. They were dealing with a very dangerous man.

And right that minute, they were no closer to finding Cole than they had been an hour before.

"Guess we're going to the party," he mumbled to himself.

EIGHT

Zach tugged on his suit coat and adjusted his tie for the hundredth time since he'd put it on fifteen minutes before. Flexing his shoulders, he tried to stretch the fabric of the too-small suit. It did no good.

He'd give all the money in his wallet—all twelve dollars—to be in even his stiffest battle dress uniform. Camo pants and a crusty T-shirt sounded a million times better than the starched cotton of his white shirt, which pulled taut across his chest and gut.

Smoothing a hand down the fabric, he tried to remember the last time he'd worn this suit. Luke's wedding. More than a year ago.

Because he hated dressing up. Dress uniform. Suit and tie. It didn't matter. He'd rather get wet and sandy than get gussied up.

"Come on, Kristi," he hollered up the stairs. "You about ready?" There was no reason for the rush. Luke and Mandy hadn't even arrived to watch Cody yet. But the sooner they left, the sooner he could take off the stupid noose around his neck.

Get in. Get the file. Get out.

It was an easy op.

But his stomach was in a knot, and his heart thud-ded like he'd run a mile in the sand.

"I'll be right there."

Cody appeared at the top of the stairs, dropping toys as he dragged his blanket across each step. "She looks really pretty. Her dress is red."

His heart gave a little kick, like he was nervous.

No. That was ridiculous. This wasn't a first date. It wasn't any kind of date.

This wasn't the fulfillment of his high school dreams or any other dreams.

It was a mission. Pure and simple.

His head accepted the words. His heart took another lurch.

Perfect. He needed a distraction.

"You need anything, little man?"

Cody shook his head and plopped onto the couch. "*First Gear* is on."

Of course. If the show was on, the kid was watching it. And the show was always on. "You hungry?"

"Nope. Still full from dinner."

Dinner. Right. Kristi had cooked a Southern chicken-salad thing. It was pretty tasty, for being 95 percent green. He swung into the kitchen and found just the diversion he needed. Both sides of the sink were filled to the brim with dirty bowls, used plates and some sort of lettuce spinner that he didn't recall owning before his last deployment.

And per usual, Kristi had cooked. And *forgotten* to clean up.

He was starting to suspect that the perpetual dirty dishes were less about forgetting and more about not wanting to tackle them.

Still, he'd rather think about the chore than Kristi's

red dress. Or playing the role of her doting husband in front of her coworkers. Or ending up under the mistletoe.

Pressing flat palms against the counter on each side of the sink, he hung his head and inhaled through his nose.

Stop it. Stop thinking about that, McCloud.

She was his wife.

But she wasn't his.

She is not yours!

He could say it over and over. It was true. His heart just hadn't caught up.

He'd vowed to honor and protect her, and he'd do whatever it took. Including denying the feelings he'd held on to for far too long.

Even though she was finally free, he wouldn't ever be the man she wanted.

He hadn't told her when they were young. He'd never confessed to his feelings because even then he'd seen her and Aaron shared something special. But she had to know—in the deepest parts of her heart—that she needed only to wave her hand to call him to her side.

And no matter how hard he pushed those feelings down, they popped up at the most inopportune moments. Like this one.

He had to remember that he was not the type of man she needed. She needed someone like Aaron. Someone gentler and softer. Someone with a kind voice and easygoing style.

The teams had made him into a lot of things. Gentler wasn't one of them.

He loved what he did. And he was good at it. He wanted to continue doing it for as long as he was physically able.

Which meant he wasn't good for her.

"I'm ready." Her words were so quiet he almost missed them. But when he looked up, he couldn't miss her.

She'd tamed her curls into a halo that glowed under the kitchen lights. Eyes shimmering, she offered him a smile as red as her dress that hugged her torso from her almost-bare shoulders until it reached her waist, where it flared. Some sort of netting poked out at her knees, and it seemed to keep her skirt dancing as she moved.

Cody slipped up behind his mom and put his arms around her. "Told you she looked pretty."

Plastering a stupid grin in place, he nodded. It was a lie. No one could call such a stunning creature merely *pretty.* But there were no words to describe the way her simple presence made his head spin.

He'd have stood there, silently gawking, all night if three solid raps on the door hadn't shaken him from his stupor. He rushed past her and greeted Luke and Mandy, quickly drawing them into the house and forcing himself to focus on anything but the porcelain sheen of Kristi's skin.

"Kristi, this is Mandy."

The brunette reached out her hand with a broad smile. "Good to meet you."

"And this is Luke."

"You're sure you don't mind watching Cody?" Kristi held out her hand, and Cody shuffled into the entryway, rubbing at the oxygen tube running across his cheek.

Luke squatted down, eye level with Cody, and pointed to the tank on his back. "Pretty cool setup you got there."

Cody lifted his eyebrows, surprise lighting his little features. "It's oxygen. It's supposed to help me stay awake. But I still fall asleep a lot."

"I like to sleep, too." Luke looked toward the television. "What are you watching?"

"First Gear."

Holding up a tight fist, Luke waited for the little guy to bump knuckles. "Love that show."

"Want to watch?" Cody led the way, and Luke followed, while Mandy waited, seeming to know that there would be more instructions.

"I just checked his oxygen pack and cannulas, so he could be fine all night, but if there's any trouble, there's a tank in the front closet." Kristi gestured toward the door behind Mandy. "We shouldn't be more than two hours, and I left my number on the fridge. I know you have Zach's number, but just in case."

Mandy's smile grew wider. "Of course."

It took another ten minutes to run through Cody's bedtime routine, the emergency contact information and the acceptable snack choices—just in case he felt like eating.

When there was no possible excuse for them to linger, Mandy gently brushed them out the door. "Have a good time. Everything will be fine. We'll see you later."

"You'll call if anything happens?"

"Of course."

Kristi didn't look convinced. Oddly enough, Zach didn't feel particularly certain either. His stomach gave a strange roll as they hurried to the car. He immediately scanned the street for a car or person out of place. There wasn't even a dog walker out in the fresh darkness, only the whisper of a breeze through the rosebushes.

With a shiver, Kristi pulled her sheer wrap over her

arms, tucking her clutch purse beneath her chin. "It's going to be okay. Right?"

"Yes." He forced himself to sound confident. "We'll get in, get what we need and get out. We can do it in forty-five minutes tops."

Forty-five minutes later Kristi was on her second glass of punch and still stuck in a conversation with her boss's wife. She hadn't gotten closer than a hundred feet from the file room. And despite surveying the partygoers for anyone watching her too closely, she'd identified exactly nothing out of the ordinary.

Across the room, she caught Zach's eye and gave him a half smile. He lifted his punch cup as Walt clapped him on the back, clearly in the middle of a story that he found hilarious. Zach gave a quick nod toward the door.

She looked where he'd directed, past half a dozen clusters of men in suits and women in party dresses. The long table and chairs had been removed from the office conference room and replaced by a handful of tall-top tables, each decorated with a sprig of holly and red berries. The lights had been dimmed, and the room buzzed with music and conversation. And everyone was distracted.

With a quick nod, Kristi confirmed that she'd meet him on the other side of the door.

"I'm going to duck into…" She hoped Veronica, Walt's wife, would connect the dots but not before Kristi could make her escape. She didn't need company to the ladies' room. She slid around the circumference of the room, dodging Quentin, who danced to the low music and smelled like his cup had something stronger than punch in it. He tried to invite her into his party-for-one, but she held up her hands and waved him off.

When she finally reached the only exit, she put her hand on the doorknob at the same moment that another hand clamped over hers. Heat raced up her arm as she swung around to zero in on Zach, who didn't say a word as he twisted her hand to open the door and slipped them into the hallway. Somehow they were halfway to the file room before she realized he hadn't let go of her hand.

The hall's darkness wrapped eerily around them. A door closed loudly, and she whipped around to make sure that no one had followed them.

The corridor was empty.

Letting out a slow breath, she tried to calm herself down. No one at the party wanted to harm her. Maybe.

Unless there was someone on Cole's payroll.

And if so, there was no telling who that might be.

Zach soothed her with a quick squeeze of her fingers as they came to the door of the file room. Kristi led the way in but couldn't risk turning on a light. He was prepared. After the door clicked closed behind them, he pulled a small flashlight from his pocket and shined it across the rows of dark gray filing cabinets.

"Our office manager is meticulous, so a file on Cole would be in with this year's other files." She pointed to a large white label on the cabinet. "Let's start here."

Zach nodded, holding up the light as she tugged on the drawer. It rattled but didn't budge.

Her stomach sank to the floor. Of course. Ginger wouldn't leave the confidential files unlocked. Especially not on a night when the office was full of guests.

Kristi squeezed her eyes closed. "I'm sorry. I should have thought. I don't have a key."

"Mind if I give it a try?"

She turned her gaze on him and spoke in a low, even tone. "It's locked."

He shrugged, stretching the fabric of his suit coat. The one that looked terribly out of place—and terribly good—on him. Again, he reached into his pocket and pulled out a tool of his trade. His hands dwarfed the little knife, but he manipulated it with unmistakable ease.

With a quick flick of his wrist, she heard a small pop, the lock releasing. Zach slid the drawer open, motioning for her to dig in.

Where had he learned that? Was it just ingrained in SEALs? Or men in general?

She shook her head, trying not to think about how often he came to her rescue. It was dangerous how much she was coming to rely on it.

She returned her focus to the drawer. The files were lined up in neat rows, all alphabetical and perfectly ordered, and she skimmed through the *A* and *B* sections before narrowing in on the *C* names. "Cartridge. Center. Cobb. Cunningham." Her fingers stopped their dance over the manila files as the beam of light jerked to indicate Zach had heard it, too. "Where's Cole?"

"Maybe it's under Jackson?"

No. But she looked anyway, swinging the top drawer closed and opening the second one.

The file wasn't there either.

She met his gaze, even as the corners of her eyes began to burn. Blinking rapidly, she wrapped her arms around her middle and squeezed tight. She hated the thought that popped to mind but couldn't stop from voicing it. "This proves that someone in the office is covering for Cole."

"Or that the file was misplaced."

She shook her head. "Ginger would never. She's too careful."

His wide palm rubbed the top of his head as he squinted, clearly lost in thought.

"Maybe a file wasn't made on him. You said he was never a client." Zach's voice rose a fraction as he laid out his theory. "Maybe Ginger never got around to making him a file. Or maybe he never gave her enough information to start one. I'm guessing that drug dealers aren't eager to pass out a lot of personal information. What's the point of a file with no information in it?"

"That's possible. I guess." Except what if he was wrong?

Suddenly the black silhouette of a man appeared on the blinds covering the window into the hallway. Her heart jumped to her throat, and she froze.

Zach didn't. In one move he turned off his flashlight, pocketed it and twirled her into his arms. Sheltered from view by the corner of the cabinet, he whispered into her ear, "Stay quiet."

Like she needed to be told. She couldn't have spoken if she'd tried.

His arm snaked around her waist, and she pressed her hands against his chest, burying her face between them. *Please, God. Get us out of here safely. Please.*

Of late her prayers had been little more than pleas for rescue, but as she snuggled deeper into Zach's embrace, she wondered if he wasn't the answer to many of them. Had God known that Zach was who she needed even back in Montana?

Undoubtedly so. And she sent up a quick prayer of thanks for the man who held her so securely.

Another set of footsteps joined the first in the hall, and then Kristi heard a loud giggle. Followed by a loud shushing and more laughter. Probably two coworkers who had had some spiked punch and were enjoying the casual atmosphere a little too much.

Zach let out a deep sigh. "They're not looking for us. But as soon as they leave, we should get back before we're missed."

"Right." Because she couldn't stay in his arms all evening. Even if she'd acted on worse ideas before.

Forcing herself to take a step away from his warmth, she paused when he reached for her face. His fingers stopped, pulled back, then stretched out again to tuck one of her unruly curls behind her ear. Heat singed through her, and she quickly covered her cheeks, lest her blush—even in the dark—give away her reaction to his innocent touch.

The couple in the hall moved on, and a door slammed somewhere deeper in the office.

"Let's go." Grabbing for her hand, he led the way to the door and stopped just long enough to peek into the darkness beyond. Satisfied, he kept moving, tugging her in his wake.

She tiptoed behind him toward the party, but just as he reached for the door, it swung open. Even the muted party lights seemed like a follow spot directly on them.

Veronica laughed and clapped from her spot just inside the room, drawing way too much attention. "I wondered where you two had gone. Now I see." Her obvious wink made Kristi's cheeks burn all over again, as every face turned a little knowing.

She hadn't stolen away for a rendezvous with her husband. She hadn't even *kissed* her husband, save for the chaste kiss on her cheek at their wedding and when he returned from his deployment.

But they didn't know that.

Zach, always so cool under pressure, joined with a chuckle and pulled her into his side in the door frame. "I sure missed her while I was gone."

That brought more laughs until someone pointed and hollered, "Look! You're under the mistletoe."

No. No. No. Her very modern coworkers wouldn't enforce such a ridiculous tradition. Would they?

"Go on, then. Kiss her like you missed her."

That sounded an awful lot like Ginger, but she didn't have time to see who had egged them on. In a single movement, Zach snagged her hand and spun her to him. She barely had time to catch herself against his chest and to register the heavy thudding of his heart beneath her palm.

"What are you doing?" she whispered.

His hazel eyes softened until they were almost green, but the smile there never quite reached his lips. Which she suddenly couldn't tear her gaze from. The curve of his bottom lip trembled. Or maybe that was her shaking as his hand cupped her elbow, his fingers warm and reassuring.

"Are you ready?"

For what?

There was no time to ask. And less time to prepare.

Electricity raced straight to her heart, then exploded to every extremity at the slightest touch of his lips to hers.

Please, let that be it. She couldn't trust her legs to keep her upright if he tried that again.

Her request went ignored, as he tilted his head, finding a better angle and pressing more firmly against her. His kiss was steady but gentle, filled with an assurance of exactly what he wanted to give—and to receive from her.

And she wanted to give it to him. Whatever that was, she prayed she had it to offer.

At some point she lost track of which heartbeat was his and which was hers as they fell into an equally wild sprint.

Someone let out a low whistle, and the spell snapped.

Kristi stumbled back, Zach's hand on her arm helping her find her footing before she embarrassed herself further.

Still, she couldn't look away from his low-watt smile. He was trying to look confident, and she was sure the crowd around them was fooled—but she'd known him too long. She recognized the tentativeness in his expression. The uncertainty. Strange, to see the shy teenager Zach McCloud in the confident man he'd become.

But another face flashed in her mind. So similar to Zach's. Deep hazel eyes and a matching cleft in his chin that their grandfather had passed down to them both.

Aaron. She'd never kissed another man. Had never had anything to compare him with.

Until now.

Neither was bad. Only…different.

Veronica gave her a playful push on the arm. "Maybe you two ought to get out of here."

Yes. Please. She just wanted to leave. They hadn't found the file they were looking for or any other information on Cole. And she'd thoroughly embarrassed herself because some idiot had thought it was a great idea to hang mistletoe at the office Christmas party.

Zach laughed and leaned in to give Veronica a quick hug. "We should get home to Cody. Thanks for a lovely party." He shook Walt's hand and clapped a couple of guys on the back before picking up her wrap.

"Enjoy your holidays," Walt called, and Kristi managed an acknowledging wave over her shoulder.

Those were the last words she heard before they settled in the car, pulled out of the parking lot and turned onto the cross street. She didn't know why Zach wasn't speaking, but she wasn't sure she could get anything coherent out of her mouth until she'd had more time to process.

That's normal after kissing your husband for the first time. Well, your second husband. In name only.

Who was she kidding? There was nothing normal about her relationship with Zach.

Or her reaction to his kiss.

Her neck burned at the memory, and she stared hard out the window, praying the twenty-minute drive could somehow be cut in half.

"Listen." His voice trailed off, and he cleared his throat without actually looking at her. "I'm sorry about that." He coughed again. "We never really talked about any of that. About—"

She cut him off before he could say it out loud. "I know. It's no big deal."

But the siren in her head and heart was blaring *Big deal. Huge deal.*

"I shouldn't have let it get so…"

Heated?

Knee-bucklingly intense?

Mind-meltingly passionate?

"…involved."

"Sure." She couldn't possibly sound any more inane if she tried.

Chancing a glance in his direction, she immediately regretted it. His profile was tense, the glow of the streetlights making his skin orange and his frown a glower.

"Obviously it was…" He trailed off, as if he wasn't sure what to call it. Was he waiting for her to fill in the blanks?

No. Nope. She was not prepared to have this conversation. Not now.

Not ever.

Suddenly her purse vibrated, and she clawed at it. For a second she let herself hope it might be the phone from the hospital, the one that meant there was a heart for Cody.

But it was her personal phone flashing an unfamiliar number. She'd accept any chance to shut down this conversation. "Hello?"

"Kristi? This is Mandy Dunham."

"Cody?"

"Is fine." Mandy's words came out smooth and confident. "He's fine. He's sleeping. But there was a situation at the house."

"I'm putting you on the speaker." She held her phone out so Zach could hear it.

"Someone tried to break in to your house tonight." Mandy rushed on. "He tried to come in through the back door, and Luke went around the house and got in a good hit before the guy took off."

"Can you identify him?" Zach asked.

The low voice had to be Luke. "He was wearing a ski mask."

Questions bubbled in Kristi's chest, and she battled between letting them free and catching her breath.

Zach didn't seem to be having the same trouble. "What was he after?"

Kristi didn't understand the question, but it seemed Luke did.

"He wasn't after your valuables. And he was surprised to see me. More surprised when I disarmed him. But he's not a pushover. He fought back."

"We're ten minutes away." The car responded as Zach pressed the gas pedal. "Make it six."

"If he wasn't trying to rob us, what did he want?" She hated the way her voice trembled. "Why was he there?"

"I don't think he was looking for you."

That made sense. He'd been a step ahead of them everywhere they went. The bridge. The hospital. The mall. Tonight wouldn't have been any different. He should have known she wouldn't be at home. Especially if he was getting information from one of her coworkers. She hadn't hidden that she was at her office party.

Which meant he wasn't looking for her. And since Zach had been very blatantly invited to the party, too, it didn't seem like the attacker was after him either. Which left...

Her stomach swung wide, and she doubled over against the bile that burned at the back of her throat.

"Kristi? Are you okay?"

She choked on a sob and nodded, then shook her head.

"It's okay. We're almost there. He's fine. He's going to be fine. No matter who's targeting—"

"Don't say it!" She knew exactly where he was going, and the thought was horrifying. It couldn't be. It wouldn't be. No one would be that cruel, that crazy.

Lacing their fingers together over the car's console, he gave her a gentle squeeze. "It'll be all right."

But how could it be when someone was trying to kill her son?

NINE

Zach called Amy Delgado first thing the next morning. Before he called Detective Diaz at the SDPD. Before he combed his hair. Before he brushed his teeth. As soon as he rolled over from a mostly sleepless night, he punched in the number to call Delgado and prayed she was a morning person.

After five rings, he was about to give up when a mumbled greeting made it across the connection.

"McCloud, I'm tagging you in my phone with a severely unhappy emoji." Apparently she'd just reached REM when the phone rang. And she wasn't happy about it. "Do you know what time it is?"

"Oh, six thirty."

"Wrong. It is precisely six nineteen."

He blinked at his alarm clock. Which he'd set eleven minutes early. "Sorry."

She sighed, mumbled something about the military and their timing and grunted. "But since you woke me up anyway, I might as well save us another delightful call later in the day."

"You got some information?"

"Just enough to know that Jackson Cole has skipped town."

Zach's gut tightened, and he leaned his elbows on his knees, perched on the edge of his bed. Was this good news? Yes, the man wouldn't be around to personally carry out any threats on Kristi...but now Zach was starting to wonder if the threat against his family came from someone else entirely. Someone with a reason to target Cody rather than Kristi.

"Since when?"

"Our best guess? Two days ago. We found out when he didn't show up for his court date yesterday—probably because every defense attorney in town turned him down. Your wife's boss wasn't the first to say no to him—or the last."

"So why would he only target Kristi?" Zach asked.

"That's the thing, Zach—I don't think he did. We don't have any indication that he's put a hit out on a civilian." She sighed like she knew it wasn't what he wanted to hear, but he gave her credit for pushing on. "I think he's probably in Mexico and most likely going to stay there for a while."

Zach bit back a groan. This info was helpful only in that it meant they'd deduced correctly. Kristi wasn't the target. And looking at the events of the past weeks in that light put a different frame on the whole situation.

The shot at the hospital hadn't been wildly off the mark. After all, he'd been carrying Cody on the same arm.

But why would anyone target a six-year-old with a heart defect? He barely had any outside interaction. He wasn't enrolled in a traditional school because he couldn't keep his eyes open long enough to make it through assignments. They didn't attend church for the same reason. His biggest outings were his regular checkups with his cardiologist.

So why Cody?

"Thank you, Amy."

"I'm sorry I couldn't be more help. Do you think your wife is going to be okay?"

Not if anything happened to Cody. "I'll figure it out." But he had no idea how.

"Listen, Drew Fortaine was in town a couple weeks back. You should give him a call. He was investigating a case. Something bad news."

"Really?" The FBI agent was another of those inter-departmental friendships he'd gained over the years. When Drew was assigned to a counterterrorism team about three years before, Zach and Jordan had been voluntold to give the feds a hand on a raid. And they'd kept in touch.

"I guess you were probably still deployed when he was here."

A half smile crept across Zach's face. "Why, Agent Delgado, have you been keeping tabs on SEAL team fifteen?"

She grumbled something low and bitter that made him laugh. Maybe she wasn't as angry with Jordan as she wanted everyone to believe. At least she cared enough to keep up with his comings and goings. "Somerton's sister told me he was gone. Anyway, it might be worth calling Drew. I think his case might be related to your situation."

"But you can't tell me about it yourself?"

"No, because I'm hoping I'm wrong."

Well, that sounded perfect. Just perfect.

"Okay. I appreciate your help. I'll give Drew a call."

And he did. It was after 6:45 a.m., which meant it was nearly ten on the East Coast. At least he wouldn't have to worry about waking up the FBI agent.

"Fortaine."

"Hey, Drew. It's Zach McCloud."

"Ziggy."

In Drew's South Carolina drawl, the nickname held little resemblance to the screams of his SEAL instructors during BUD/S—Basic Underwater Demolition/ SEAL Training—but Zach responded anyway. "I heard you were in my neck of the woods a few weeks back."

"Sure was. Sorry I missed you. I heard you were still abroad."

Zach gave a noncommittal grunt. He wasn't in the habit of confirming or denying anywhere he'd been in the last seven years.

Except, he'd told Kristi. Not a lot. Just enough to give her a peek into his life on the teams. Maybe it was because he'd wanted someone to share with. More likely he was trying to show her the truth of his reality. It wasn't a safe job. And he wasn't a safe man.

That was neither here nor there, so he pushed it aside. "I was just talking with Amy Delgado. She said you were doing some digging while you were here."

"Always digging, man. You know, they should issue shovels at Quantico. Sometimes that's about all we do."

Zach couldn't find the question he wanted to ask, so he stood and paced the narrow confines of his room to shake the words loose. "I know you can't comment on an active investigation—"

"I don't have an active investigation in California right now."

That stopped him midstride. "You don't?"

"No, I do not." Smooth as melted butter. But there was a hint of a question in his tone.

"Then can you tell me what you were looking into?"

"Can you tell me why?"

Zach took a step. Stopped. Then took another. "Someone's been targeting my family."

"Your folks? They still in Texas?"

"No. Not my parents. My wife and—" well, there was just no other word for it "—my son."

Drew sounded like he was choking. "Wait a minute. You got married? When did this happen?"

This was not the conversation he wanted to have. No way was he going to explain the ins and outs of his rather unconventional marriage.

"We grew up together. It's not a big deal."

"I beg to differ. This is a very big deal."

"It's really not." Zach forced himself to keep his tone level, even as he laced it with steel. "What I need to know is what brought an FBI agent all the way from DC to San Diego to work a case."

Drew's tone instantly shifted as he realized they weren't talking in generalities or what-if scenarios. This was real life and a real threat against people Zach really cared about.

"There was an attempted kidnapping of a ten-year-old girl in El Centro."

Zach had never been to the town, but he'd seen it on enough maps. It was only a couple of hours outside San Diego, straight east on I-8.

"Attempted?"

"Yeah. The girl was grocery shopping with her mom. As they exited the store, a van pulled up, and a man grabbed the girl's arm and tried to pull her into the cargo bay."

He rubbed against a fire in his chest as he imagined the mom's fear. As he thought about Kristi's. "You said *attempted*."

"A police officer was there, making his usual rounds.

He saw what was happening, rammed his patrol car into the front of the van hard enough to distract the kidnapper, I guess. The girl popped out and ran to her mother."

"Why call in a special agent?"

"The van was spotted crossing into Arizona, so I was digging up any information I could find to make sure they hadn't found another victim."

Zach tried to release the tension that had turned his shoulders into a knotted mess, but he had a feeling that Drew hadn't told him the whole story. "What happened to the girl?"

Silence.

After a long moment, Drew cleared his throat. "There was an accident about three weeks ago. She was driving with her dad, and witnesses say that three black vans surrounded the car."

It took only an instant to be back on the Coronado Bridge, to feel the fear as the beasts rolled into place around him, blocked him in. He'd found an exit strategy.

The girl's dad had not.

"The car was pushed through the guardrail, went over the edge and slammed into a tree."

"She didn't make it." It wasn't really a question, but the words were hard to get past the clog in his throat.

"No. Her dad survived. A few broken ribs and a concussion, but she was DOA when the paramedics got there."

That could have been him, Kristi and Cody. One wrong move and he would have lost Kristi and Cody both.

That swift, sure knowledge stole his breath and froze his mind.

"Zig? You okay?"

"Sure. Yeah." Maybe not really. But he would be. He

had to be. And he had just one more question. "Drew, there must be at least four FBI field offices in California and hundreds of qualified agents. Why'd they call you?"

"Special circumstances."

His heart slammed into his ribs as icy fingers wrapped around his neck. Somehow, deep inside, he knew the answer before he asked the question. "What special circumstances?"

"She had a heart condition. She was at the top of the transplant list."

"Kristi, I need to talk with you. Alone."

She jumped at the thread of iron running through Zach's voice. In her lap, Cody groaned, his eyes remaining closed.

"Sure. Hang on." She tried to reposition Cody on the couch with minimal disruption, but her hands were already shaking, worrying over why Zach might be so upset so early in the morning.

After the realization the night before that Cody might be the real target of these attacks, she'd slept on the floor of his room, always with a hand on his arm. And even now, she let her fingers trail to his elbow, not quite ready to let him out of her sight. Even if Zach was leading her only to the kitchen.

Zach leaned a hip against the counter, looking big and intimidating with his arms crossed over his chest. She hovered in the open entry, always with a clear view of the couch and Cody's blanket.

Apparently Zach decided the distance between them was unacceptable, as he shuffled closer. When their eyes met, she saw pain there. For her? For Cody? She couldn't tell.

But she was certain she was going to hate whatever bomb he was about to drop.

"According to the DEA, Jackson Cole isn't after anyone in San Diego right now. He missed his court date, skipped bail and is hiding out—probably somewhere in Mexico."

That wasn't bad news. In fact, it was enough to let her take a deep breath. A real breath. No one else had a reason to come after them. They were safe. They had to be.

"That's great…isn't it?"

"But that's not all."

He cleared his throat, and it was just enough time for her stomach to plummet to her toes.

Zach's eyes narrowed as he reached for her arm, apparently thought better of it and dropped his hand to his side. "A few weeks ago a little girl from El Centro was almost kidnapped."

"Almost?" Her voice wavered, but she pushed on. "She escaped?"

"A cop saw what was happening, and he was able to foil the abduction."

The pieces still weren't fitting together. "Why are you telling me this? What does it have to do with us?"

"She was a heart patient."

"Was?" The croaked syllable was all she could manage.

Zach seemed to understand what she couldn't even say she needed. Scooping her into his arms, he held her tight enough that she could feel the break in his voice when he finally went on. "She was killed in a car accident a few days later. Her dad was forced off the road and hit a tree."

Tears leaked down her cheeks, and she wanted to wipe them away, but her arms were pinned between

Zach's chest and her own. She didn't even know this little girl's name, but her heart ached for the girl's parents, for her friends.

"Was she close—to getting a heart?"

"At the top of the list."

"Why-y?" Her voice cracked, and she hiccupped a sob before continuing. "Why would someone do that?"

He shook his head, his stubbled cheek catching against the top of her hair. "I don't know. It could be anything. Personal vendetta against the hospital. A madman. But I don't think it's a coincidence that Cody's on that list, too."

"He killed her."

He seemed to know the question she couldn't ask, so he rushed to answer it. "I'm not going to let that happen to you and Cody. We're going to make it through this. Together."

She sighed into the word, letting it weave its comfort and hope around her heart. She wasn't in this alone. God had sent her just the man she needed for this terrifying season.

"What are we going to do?"

"We'll start with the police. They need to know what we're facing. And we may not be the only ones. Then we're going to talk with the transplant coordinator."

"Denise Engle? Why her?"

Zach ran his hands up and down her arms, building warmth and waking up her muscles. "Maybe she's noticed that her transplant list is dwindling. Maybe she's noticed something else. At the very least, she can alert other families that they're in danger."

If the look on her pale face was any indication, Denise Engle was surprised to see the McCloud family march into her office unannounced and unscheduled

later that day. But Kristi didn't have the energy for niceties. Not after the police had admitted that all they could
do was send a patrol car past the house a few times a
day. Not after the crime lab came back with zero leads
from the bomb. With no leads on who had killed Greta
Gammer, the little girl from El Centro, there was little
the police could do but wait for another attack.

Someone was going to help them. Not finding the
man after her son wasn't an option.

Kristi closed the door behind them with a decisive
click and plopped down in one of the two chairs in front
of the desk. Zach sat with a lighter touch, although his
arms were full of a sprawled-out six-year-old.

Denise quickly schooled her features. "To what do
I owe this surprise?"

Kristi stared hard at the other woman. "What do you
know about Greta Gammer?"

Denise's brown eyes flashed with a mix of shock and
horror, and all the color drained from her face.

"How do you know about Greta?"

Kristi glanced at Zach, suddenly not sure she could
say the words out loud. But when he gave her an encouraging nod, she took a steadying breath and turned
back to Denise.

"We think whoever targeted Greta has moved on
to Cody."

Her jaw hung slack for what felt like a full minute,
her eyes blinking rapidly the whole time. "What do you
mean, *targeted*? Wasn't it a car accident?"

"It was a car crash—but not an accident. Eyewit-
ness reports say the car was deliberately driven off the
road. And days before that, she was nearly kidnapped."

Denise's swallow reverberated through the tiny office, and her gaze swung to the wall where a cluster

of four pictures commemorated a party. Denise with a silver-haired woman and a younger man in front of a cruise ship. Denise laughing with a mustachioed man. The same man hugging a little girl.

Then Denise hung her head. "I don't know what's happening. Except that the police have been in touch."

Zach spoke for the first time, low enough not to disturb Cody but forceful enough to demand an answer. "With you? With others on the transplant list?"

"They called me a couple weeks ago. They wanted the other names on the transplant list. But I couldn't give it to them."

"You didn't give the police the list?" She tried to keep the astonishment out of her voice, but she couldn't figure out what this woman had been thinking. She knew there might have been an issue, and she hadn't helped the cops? "Why not?"

"HIPAA regulations. If I were to reveal the names on the list, I'd be violating all sorts of federal privacy laws. I'd lose my job, and I could face years in prison. I think they've put in a request for a court order, but these things take some time. HIPAA isn't a joke."

Maybe not, but this conversation was starting to feel like one. Kristi inhaled deeply, then let out a slow breath between tight lips.

And because Zach seemed to know just when to step in, he said, "To your knowledge, has anyone else on the list been attacked?"

"No. No one but Greta. And then…"

Kristi pressed flat hands on the polished edge of the wood desk. "What?"

"When I heard he was shot—" she nodded toward Zach "—I wondered if… It just seemed like too much of a coincidence."

Coincidence. Sure. Denise could keep telling herself that if it made her feel better. But Kristi couldn't help but think if she'd worked more with the police, maybe they'd have been able to keep a bomb from showing up in her kitchen.

She felt like she'd fall apart until Zach slipped his hand into hers and gave it a gentle squeeze.

"Why didn't you say something to us?" he asked.

She hadn't thought it was possible, but Denise turned even whiter. "I—I wasn't sure exactly what happened. And I couldn't tell the cops without revealing that Cody is on the list."

"If you'd told me what was going on, *I'd* have told the cops we were on the list." She hadn't meant to spit the words out quite so harshly, and she bit her tongue to keep from going on.

God, give me kinder words. Right now all I have is confusion and anger. And so much frustration.

Denise shrank back, slouching in her office chair. Her eyes shifted rapidly back and forth as if she was looking for the right excuse. "It's my job to protect those names."

"Maybe you should spend more time remembering that those names belong to real people with real families." Kristi pushed herself to her feet and towered over Denise. "They're not *just* names on your list."

As he joined her, Zach's eyes narrowed. "Besides, based on the way kids have already been targeted, it's clear that at least one other person got a hold of that list."

TEN

Zach sat in the car for several minutes, letting Kristi's rapid breathing slowly return to normal and the flush covering her face begin to fade. He gripped the steering wheel until his hands no longer shook and the throbbing in his head faded to a dull ache.

He hadn't felt this way in a long time—maybe ever. He had no idea what to do next. Just an urge that whatever he did needed to be done. Now.

With a quick glance into the backseat, he confirmed that Cody was still sacked out. Then he let his gaze settle on Kristi, whose head rested against the back of the seat, her eyes open and focused on the sun visor, probably still chewing on the news about the list.

He tossed around several conversation starters, but none of them seemed to fit. Anyway, the starter didn't matter nearly as much as the final direction.

And that was still a blank.

The cops were tied up in red tape without a pair of scissors.

Denise wasn't going to share any more information than she already had.

And there was still someone after Cody.

No way was he going to let his family sit out there

like bait for a rabid wolf. But what could he do to protect them when he didn't know which way to look to find the source of the danger?

"I guess maybe I got a little hot in there. Sorry about that."

Kristi's announcement caught him off guard and made him chuckle. "I don't think anyone would blame you."

"Well, Denise probably isn't going to mark our upcoming appointments with a heart on her calendar."

He snorted at the visual. "Probably not."

"So what are we going to do?"

He closed his eyes and prayed for some direction, a clear thought. If only there was an obvious turn for them to take. But they'd followed every lead to a dead end. Every one, except one.

His chest tightened at the very thought, but once it had formulated, he couldn't let it go. "What about Greta's parents?"

She didn't look nearly as interested as he was. "What about them?"

He shrugged. "Maybe they saw or heard something. What if they did their own PI work? Maybe they have a lead that's stuck with the El Centro cops that never made it to the SDPD."

Her brown eyes turned liquid as her lips pinched together. "They just lost their child. We can't storm into their lives and ask them to relive that on the chance that they *might* have some information."

Reaching for her hand, he shot another glance into the backseat, and her gaze followed his. "What if the situation were reversed? What if Cody had been taken from you, and you had a chance to help out a frantic mother? Would you turn her away just because it hurt to think about him?"

It took her barely a blink to respond. "I'll get the address. You get us on the road."

This team thing was new, and it made his heart ache in the sweetest way.

Of course, he'd spent years working with men who were closer than brothers, men he trusted absolutely. From his swim buddy at BUD/S to the guys on his team, he was never alone, never really on his own. As long as he was working, he was watching someone's six—making sure no one crept up behind them—and he trusted that someone was watching his.

But when he was home, he was alone. On leave, he wasn't exactly isolated; he just flew solo.

Chores. Cooking. Cleaning. It was all up to him. Until it wasn't anymore—thanks to Kristi.

Granted, no one ever left dirty dishes in his sink before. But they also never made him delicious meals. Or made room for him on the couch next to a sleepy little boy who grinned at him like he was a superhero. Or held his hand when he needed it most.

Kristi's fingers were narrow and soft, but she held on to him with a strength that ran to her very core. Sure, she was emotional. She was also unafraid to show him that side of her. And she was resilient and assured. She was kind and funny. Thoughtful and fiercely protective of Cody. And of him.

And right now, for a moment he could hold her hand, offer her comfort and enjoy simply being with her.

He hadn't even known he was lonely until he realized how full this little family made his life. They filled an emptiness he'd never recognized before.

In the back of his mind, he could hear his Bible study

teacher leading a discussion on the book of Ecclesiastes and a reminder that "two are better than one. For if either of them falls, the one will lift up his companion."

Zach had always known that to be true on the teams.

But apparently there was an application to his home life, too.

Just not with Kristi.

He swallowed the bitter taste that always accompanied that reminder. He'd keep telling himself that truth as long as it took. No matter how much he liked having her and Cody around, he wasn't the right kind of man for them, and he wasn't ever going to be.

Letting himself care too much was just asking for heartache.

As they neared the outlet mall on the metro area's farthest outskirts, a quiet voice from behind him snapped Zach to attention.

"I'm hungry. Can we get chicken nuggets?"

Zach looked at Kristi, and they both laughed. The day had flown by so fast that they hadn't bothered to stop for a meal break.

"Sure, little man. Let's get some food."

The stop didn't last more than twenty minutes. Just long enough to order, eat and wash up. While the food seemed to perk Cody up, Zach worried that he might not have the stamina to make the four-hour round trip. But there wasn't anything else to be done. With Cody in danger, he wasn't about to leave the boy with a sitter, nor was he going to send Kristi all the way to El Centro by herself. Not when their pursuer had proven time and again that he wasn't afraid of collateral damage.

Sticking together was their only option. If Cody could hold on through the trip.

He caught Kristi's gaze and nodded toward the little

man, asking with his eyes. She mouthed her response. "He'll be okay."

They passed the rest of the drive in near silence, Zach as lost in his own thoughts as Kristi seemed to be in hers. He tried to imagine what an interaction with the Gammers might be like. But all he could picture was a stone wall of silence and a slammed door in their faces.

Kristi directed him into a small subdivision of cookie-cutter homes, each as pale and sun weary as the one before. The Gammer home was as unremarkable as every other one on the block. Single-story ivory stucco with faded brown trim. The lawn might have been green at one point, but now it was mostly dirt.

Zach pulled up in front of the home and turned off the car. The lack of air-conditioning was immediately apparent—even in December—under the unrelenting sun. Kristi reached for her door, but an instinct made Zach grab her hand. "Wait. Just a second." She turned back with raised eyebrows, and he shrugged. It was hard to know if his apprehension was due to the meeting they were about to have or if he'd sensed that someone had followed them. Maybe the low-level tingling on the back of his neck would just be a part of life as long as someone was after Cody.

He needed a calmer spirit, and he knew only one way to get that. Dipping his head, he whispered, "Lord, keep us safe. Give us the right questions. Let the Gammers be open to answering them."

Kristi squeezed his hand, and when he looked up, there was a full smile on her lips. "Thank you."

He nodded and led the way, gathering Cody and his toy car, before making his way up the cement walkway.

Kristi raised her fist and rapped on the wooden door

three times. A dog barked inside, but no one opened the door.

Kristi shot him a questioning look, and he lifted a shoulder. He guessed if he was in their shoes, he wouldn't want unannounced visitors either. "Try again."

She did. The barking came from farther back in the house this time.

Maybe they needed something a little more forceful. With the heel of his fist, Zach gave the door two solid thumps. It rattled the heavy wood and adjacent window.

Kristi's eyes opened wider, and she covered her mouth with her hand, like she was trying to subdue another smile. He winked at her, wishing he could tell her to never hide her smile. It was one of his favorite things about her, and at the moment they could use any joy to be found.

Suddenly the blinds at the window flickered, and a woman appeared there. She probably wasn't much older than Kristi, but grief had hollowed her cheeks and sunk her red-rimmed eyes. "Go away!" she yelled, her voice muted through the glass.

Zach shook his head quickly. "We need your help!"

"No!" The blinds flicked closed.

Kristi's nose wrinkled, and her lips pinched together. "Maybe we should have called first."

Maybe. But that would have given the Gammers a chance to shut them down long-distance. It would be harder to refuse them eye-to-eye.

After readjusting Cody's position in his arms, Zach gave the door three more thumps and pressed the door-bell, which gave a pitiful thunk.

Suddenly the front door swung open, and a thin man with blazing brown eyes lit into them. "Whatever you're selling, we're not interested. Whatever you want, we can't help. Go away." He moved to slam the door.

With barely a moment to consider his options, Zach wedged his foot in the way.

The man scowled. "I'm calling the cops."

Kristi rushed between them, holding up her hands. "Please. Wait. Please. Just hear us out."

Branden Gammer looked doubtful as he pushed his hand through his shaggy hair and eyed Zach.

"My son needs a heart transplant," Kristi explained.

Branden's nostrils flared.

"We think someone is trying to kill him."

Gammer turned white and loosened his grip on the door.

"We think that maybe the same someone targeted your daughter." Kristi's voice was soft, filled with an empathy that only a grieving parent could truly share.

Branden's gaze swooped on Cody's resting form and the oxygen pack he carried. "Greta had one of those, too. The doctor said she was going to have to move to the hospital full-time, but that was before…"

Mrs. Gammer—Toni—slipped under her husband's arm, holding him tight as she eyed Kristi with suspicion. "What is it that you want from us? Our girl is gone."

"I am so sorry for your loss." Kristi pressed her hand to Cody's back. "We just hoped you might be able to help us. We've run out of ideas, and someone is still coming after Cody."

The Gammers stared at each other for a long, silent moment, and Zach held his breath as they considered. He couldn't pray hard enough or fast enough that God would soften their hearts. It was clear that their grief was still raw, but he prayed that they would put themselves in Kristi's shoes and find the grace to help.

Finally Toni turned to them. "I don't know what we could tell you that would help, but maybe you should come in." She stepped back, and after a long beat of silence, her husband opened the door wide enough for them to enter.

Zach followed Kristi into the living room. Two oversize leather couches dominated the square space. Fast-food wrappers and empty glasses covered the slate coffee table, which looked like it hadn't been cleaned off in weeks. It was about what he'd expect for a man and woman lost in grief.

"How did you find us?" Branden asked as he settled onto a couch, motioning that Zach and Kristi should do the same.

When Kristi lifted her brown eyes toward him, Zach offered a pained smile. There's no story better than the truth. Or so his dad always said.

"I'm Zach McCloud." He patted himself on the chest. "This guy is Cody, and this is my wife, Kristi."

She shivered at his side, and he wondered if she was responding to his use of the term. Yes, she was his *wife*. But the introduction never got any less strange.

He pushed forward. "We live in San Diego. I'm with the navy."

As often happened when he introduced himself like that, his audience let out a little sigh. Toni, who had been perched on the edge of the couch as though looking for an excuse to bolt, relaxed. Her husband put his hand on her knee, and some of the ice in his posture melted.

"When I came back from my last deployment, we were nearly run off the Coronado Bridge." He kept his gaze glued on their faces, searching for a way to get through to them. "By three black vans."

Branden's eyes flew open, and his hand flew to a spot at his side. Most likely where he'd sustained broken ribs. "Big ones? With fully tinted windows?"

Zach agreed quickly, and Toni's gaze ping-ponged back and forth between them, her eyes filled with something akin to fear.

"They maneuvered you to the side?" her husband asked. Zach gave a silent nod, and Branden continued, his eyes focused on a wall in the distance. "Then they were in front and behind." At some point in his trembling story, he'd moved from asking about Zach's experience to retelling his own. "It felt like they were everywhere. I tried to slow down, but the one behind me rammed into us. Greta was screaming, so I swerved away from the guardrail. Thought maybe I could get the van to my left to move over." He swallowed, closed his eyes and grabbed for his wife's hand. "But it didn't budge. Then suddenly the railing was gone, and we were over the edge, flying down the embankment before we slammed into the tree."

The story and every ounce of pain it carried hung over everyone in the room.

"I'd let Greta sit in the front seat with me. But her air bag didn't deploy." Branden's voice cracked and trailed off as Toni pressed his hand to her chest, tears dripping down her cheeks.

Kristi's eyes glistened, too, and she moved her hand to Zach's knee. She seemed to need the reminder that she wasn't alone listening to this story. He needed it, too.

"We're so sorry for your loss," Kristi said for the second time.

"Why would someone come after Greta?" Toni asked. "She was such a sweet girl, always laughing and reading, and she had so many friends when she was in school."

Toni's gentle sob nearly undid Zach, and he squeezed a sleeping Cody a little bit harder, thanking God for another day with him, another chance to rescue him.

"We hoped that if we compared notes, we might be able to find a pattern. A reason."

Branden nodded and launched into the story of the attempted kidnapping. It wasn't anything that Drew hadn't already told Zach, but he listened intently anyway. The details were all the same. The store. The parking lot. The van. The cop.

Branden filled in the timeline from the attempted kidnapping to the accident to this moment. But it wasn't new information. The FBI and local police had all of it.

And were coming up empty-handed in finding the person responsible, too.

That realization ate at Zach's gut, taunting him. He couldn't do more than dig up outdated information and run when they were being chased. It was a poor excuse for a mission if ever he'd seen one.

"And you're sure there was nothing else strange or out of the ordinary that you noticed leading up to the attacks?"

Toni shook her head. "I don't think so. You must know. Those first months after the diagnosis—well, it was hard to remember my own name let alone what was going on with Greta."

"Sure." If she tried to hide the disappointment in her voice, Kristi failed. With slumped shoulders and a distinct quivering in her lower lip, she scooted to the edge of the couch. "Well, then. Thank you for—"

Branden held up his hand. "There was one thing."

Toni looked surprised. "What thing?"

Branden's gaze shifted to the floor as hope bubbled in Zach's chest. He began to squeeze Kristi's hand, but she beat him to it.

"I thought it was a joke. A sick one, but harmless." He raised a shoulder in a stiff shrug as Toni glared at him through narrowed eyes. Meeting his wife's gaze, he tried to explain. "You were already so stressed. I just thought you didn't need something else on your plate, so I didn't tell you."

"What?" The word was barely a breath, but it held a world of emotions—at the forefront, anger.

"There was a phone call. Maybe a month before the attempted kidnapping."

Everything stilled. Even the dog, who had been barking, seemed to understand the need for silence. Zach prayed that this might be the clue they needed.

His mouth went dry, but he managed to prod the stalled story. "What kind of call?"

"A man said he was a lawyer. He wouldn't give the name of his client, but he said the man wanted…" Branden shifted awkwardly in his seat. "He wanted the heart."

"What heart?" Kristi asked.

"The one that would have been Greta's. He said he'd pay—two million dollars."

Toni's mouth hung open, her eyes wide and unblinking, her body utterly motionless.

Even Kristi was stunned silent. Zach found his voice first. "This lawyer's client wanted to buy Greta's new heart?"

"Yes. But it would have meant a death sentence for my daughter. I—I thought he was joking. I mean, who would even suggest something like that?" Branden caught Toni's chin and angled it toward himself. "I told him it wasn't funny and not to call again."

"And did he?" Zach said.

"Call? No. Never. But, you don't really think it's related, do you? He couldn't have been serious. Could he?"

"Actually…" Zach pursed his lips to the side and tried to figure out how to be honest without scaring Kristi or the Gammers. "I don't think it was a joke. He wanted that heart. He still *wants* a heart."

He didn't have to connect the dots for anyone else in the room. Branden and Toni hugged each other as tears streamed down their cheeks. Now they knew why their daughter had been killed.

Kristi nudged Zach's knee. "We should go."

He nodded, and they tried to slip out without disturbing the grieving couple. But right as they reached the door, Branden caught up with them. Slipping a white business card into Zach's hand, he said, "Keep in touch. Let us know when you catch the scum who's doing this."

Zach nodded, shook the man's hand and followed Kristi into the late-afternoon sunshine.

When they reached the car, Kristi didn't climb into the passenger seat. Instead, she followed Zach to the driver's side and watched as he put Cody into his booster seat.

Leaning her hip against the side of the car, she said, "Could someone really be trying to kill the kids at the top of the transplant list? Why would anyone do that?"

He looked up at her and shook his head. "I think it's just what he told Branden in that call. He wants the next available heart." It didn't make sense, though. If a man needed that heart so badly, he'd be on a list to receive it, right?

Zach dropped his gaze back into the interior of the car and stooped to pick up the stuffed toy that Cody had dropped on the floorboard.

Kristi said something else, but her words were lost to the sudden rushing through his ears. His lungs seized, and a lump lodged in his throat.

A thin black wire ran along the edge of the carpeting before moving upward and disappearing beneath the seat. It wasn't part of the car, and it certainly hadn't been there when they'd left San Diego.

His heart took up an erratic rhythm, even as he told himself to stay calm. *Find the destination. Find the threat.*

Only he didn't need to. All of a sudden, he knew. It was under Cody's booster seat. Once again the little boy was the target of a madman.

Zach's fingers were already scrambling to release the seat belt before he could scream at Kristi to get moving. "Run!"

"What?" She frowned like she'd heard but couldn't understand his command. She was frozen in place, and Zach didn't have time to explain. The device under the booster seat might have been triggered by Cody's weight, which meant it could go off at any second. He needed his family as far away from the car as soon as possible.

With Cody in one arm, he scooped Kristi off her feet with his other and raced for the house.

Kristi squirmed, her confusion clear in her tone. "What's going on? Wha—?"

He kept running until he'd rounded the corner behind the protection of the house. Swinging them in front of him onto the ground, he tried to shield them with his own body.

Just in time.

The force of the explosion sent them flying.

ELEVEN

Kristi couldn't stop shaking.

Not when Zach scuttled over to her, pulled her into his arms and kissed her forehead before running his hands up and down her arms to check for scrapes or breaks.

Not when Toni and Branden burst out of their house to check on them.

Not even when the police arrived, red and blue lights flashing and sirens wailing.

She could tell that they were talking at her, but all she could hear was the explosion.

One of the paramedics had helped her to her feet, but her legs had refused to hold her. So she'd crawled to Cody. Of course, he was fascinated with the fire engine and ambulance—oblivious to the fact that they'd very nearly been killed.

But she couldn't stop shaking, couldn't stop envisioning a moment where Zach hadn't realized the problem in time.

Zach must have handled explaining the situation to the police and arranging for a rental car. Kristi was aware of none of it. Yet somehow when she looked up from combing the grass out of Cody's hair, there was a bright blue SUV sitting at the curb.

She couldn't find a single word to say the whole drive back to San Diego, but neither could she close her eyes and find any rest. Every time she so much as blinked, she saw her car in flames and felt the force of the blast throwing them around as if they were tumbleweeds in the wind.

It seemed to take days to get home, the setting sun always in front of them, always glaring into the car. Zach had donned his aviator sunglasses and was both silent and thoughtful. While she tried to wipe her memory altogether, Zach's jaw worked as if he was physically chewing on the events of the day.

From the backseat, Cody's video game—a gift from the Gammers—beeped and booped until she was sure it was just part of the sound of the road.

She wasn't aware of drifting off until she looked up and saw that they were pulling up to the house.

"I must have dozed off."

She wasn't entirely sure she'd spoken aloud until Zach responded. "Definitely."

What did that mean? "How do you know I wasn't just resting my eyes?"

He shot her a grin that was wholly at odds with frantic escapes and exploding cars. "You were snoring."

Embarrassment flooded through her, and she responded without even thinking. "I was not."

"If you say so." His mouth twisted into a mock serious frown, and she couldn't see his eyes to read what he was really thinking.

Rolling her eyes, she opened the door and trudged to the house. Her limbs felt like they'd doubled in size, her joints stiff like they'd forgotten how to work. She waited until Zach checked the door to make sure they weren't walking in on another trap before going inside, then fell to the couch, sapped of strength. She turned to reach for Cody, but Zach was already a third of the way up the stairs. "I can get him," she called. But the words were as sluggish as she felt, and Zach chuckled.

"I've got it covered."

She didn't argue. The couch wrapped around her, holding her in place and promising a relief from the pounding behind her eyes. But it never came. As she stared at the far wall, the knot inside only grew tighter. Eventually a flood of tears let loose, and her hiccuping sobs—while silent—racked her whole body.

"Whoa there." From nowhere Zach was by her side, crawling onto the couch, putting his arm around her back, letting her rest her head on his shoulder. "It's okay. It's all right. We'll make it through this."

His words rumbled on top of her head, sweet and soothing. And she leaned into his warmth. His chest was firm but comforting. There was something in his strength and kindness that made her insides flutter like they hadn't since she was fifteen. Since she'd fallen in love with Aaron.

But this was different. She wasn't a child anymore, with everything fresh and exciting.

This was somehow familiar but altogether new. And more terrifying than thrilling.

She couldn't deny that his presence pulled her back from a precipice she couldn't name. As the panic ebbed, she heaved a loud sigh. "I've never…"

"Seeing an explosion is a little different from having a bomb in your house, huh?"

She nodded. "Yes. We were so close. Cody was so close."

A frown worked its way across his face. "I know. But we're all okay. Everyone made it home safely. And it was a useful trip."

"It was?" They'd learned that Cody was definitely the target. How could that be useful if they still didn't know who was after him?

"Sure."

Her mind suddenly caught up. "Right. Because now we have even more of a reason to push for the transplant list from Denise. I'm going to call her."

Zach opened his mouth, then snapped it closed, clearly changing his mind about whatever he had been about to say. "Go for it," he replied. "I'm going to do a little research."

She forced herself off the couch and found her phone in her purse. Denise didn't answer, so she left a short but emphatic message. "We're sure Cody is the target because of his heart. And we need to warn the other families near the top of the list. Call me back as soon as possible."

As she hung up the phone, a yawn cracked her jaw, and she eyed the stairs. Her bed called so loudly that it was almost audible. But a quick peek at Zach piqued her curiosity. He sat in the same spot where she'd left him, but he'd picked up his laptop and was rapidly scrolling and clicking. Whatever was on the screen had captured his full interest.

"What are you looking at?"

He didn't look up but nodded toward the seat she'd vacated. "Come take a look."

She slipped into her spot and pressed into his arm to get a view of the screen.

Sure. That's why she was leaning so heavily against him.

She'd just keep telling herself that.

"So I got to thinking about that phone call that Branden got." The short whiskers on his jaw shone in the overhead light as he spoke. She felt the urge to run her finger across his cheek and explore the angles, ridges and cleft right in the center of his chin.

That wasn't safe. At all.

Wherever these feelings were coming from, she had to shut them down. She couldn't afford to be distracted from caring for Cody.

Besides, Aaron…

Had been gone for more than two years.

She no longer expected him to walk through the front door. Not since they'd left Montana.

But a piece of her heart cried out that the butterflies and breathless moments with Zach might be disloyal to her husband. That she never should have let him kiss her. That she absolutely should not have thrilled in that moment as she had. And that she most certainly should not want him to kiss her again. Although she did. A lot.

"He said the guy on the phone was a lawyer who represented an anonymous client."

She jerked her chin in an affirmative, trying to focus on his theory and not on the things she had no business thinking about.

"Doesn't that sound like something a rich guy would do?"

"I guess."

"I mean, we know the guy who wants the heart offered two million dollars. He didn't try to bargain or make an emotional appeal—he went straight to money. Only someone who's used to money fixing any problem would do that."

The pieces were falling into place like that video game Cody loved. "You think this guy wasn't bluffing about the two million—that he really had access to that much cash and would have paid out if the Gammers had agreed?"

"Yes, I think so." He pointed at the computer, which displayed the front page of the local newspaper. "And I'm guessing that a man with that kind of money and an obvious interest in heart transplants might have made a donation. A public one."

"So you're hunting for this guy in the newspaper."

Zach lifted a shoulder. "It's the only thing I could think of. Maybe there's an article about a fund-raiser or something like that. Maybe there's a name we recognize or a picture of three black vans." He tried for a smile, which faltered on his bad joke. "I'm tired of waiting for someone else to find the next lead." His eyes seemed to simmer as his gaze zeroed in on her. "I'm not going to sit back while my family is at risk."

Family.

She hadn't thought about it, but they were. An unusual one to be sure. But Zach had put his life on the line more than once for her and Cody, and she never doubted his vow to guard them. Her strong, kind, protective husband. He'd become family. And not just on paper.

Somewhere deep in her heart.

When the urge hit her, she didn't second-guess it. With a quick burst forward, she pressed her lips to his cheek in a quick kiss. As she settled her head onto his shoulder, she asked, "Why are you doing this for us?"

Zach lost his train of thought, his words and the normal rhythm of his heart.

Why? Why had he gone to Montana to propose in the first place? Why had he given up his neat and or-

dered life in favor of something that more closely resembled chaos? Why had he taken a bullet that had been
intended for Cody? And why was he so sure he'd do it
again given the same situation?

There was no casual response to such a loaded question. Especially not following a chaste kiss on his cheek
that had him feeling things he'd sworn he never would.

Her eyebrows pulled together until two little lines
appeared between them, as though she expected something from him.

Right. She was waiting on his answer.

Why? Why indeed.

Clearing his throat, he scrambled through the re-
cesses of his mind for the right answer. For the truth.
Just not the whole truth.

Nope. The whole truth would scare her.

It scared *him*.

Mostly it scared him that someday he might not be
able to keep it in check and he'd act on it.

"Well, you needed me. Or at least a place to stay and
access to better health care. I've known you since I was
thirteen, and Aaron would have wanted me to watch
out for you and Cody. How could I not?"

Her eyes narrowed like she was trying to see through
him. And maybe she was succeeding.

She knew. She had to. She could see it on his face,
in his eyes, in the way he couldn't keep his hands still.
She could hear it in the hammering of his heart.

She'd figured out the truth, that he'd been in love
with her since he was sixteen. Maybe she'd known all
along. While it was never stated, it must have been obvious that she had only to voice her choice and she could
have had either of them.

Zach was the wild summer visitor, Aaron the boy next door.

But it had always been clear that Kristi preferred Aaron's soft-spoken bearing to Zach's rumble-tumble ways. She liked his stability and temperate demeanor.

Zach had gotten into a hotheaded fight or two and ended up with a black eye more than once. He hadn't known how to be like Aaron.

He still didn't. Even though that's what she needed.

Which meant he wasn't the one she needed.

For the moment, in the danger, he might be enough. He could protect her until they figured out who was after her. Maybe God had brought them together again because she needed him at the moment. Twelve years ago, he'd been sure that God was telling him to wait, showing him that the time wasn't right.

Now he knew it never would be. She needed him now. But when this whole mess was over, she'd need a different kind of man. Letting himself really care for her, truly falling in love again, was a disaster waiting to happen. A broken heart waiting in the wings.

So why had he come to her rescue?

Because he didn't want to forget that he'd been in love with her once.

Even if he couldn't afford to do it again.

"It's what I do," he said with a shrug. "I help the people who need it."

Pinching her lips like she still doubted his reasoning, she finally nodded. "Well…thank you. I should have said that sooner."

"You could have written me back." The words popped out unbidden and unplanned, and he wished he could shove them back inside when she yanked her head off his shoulder and covered her mouth. "I'm sorry. I didn't mean to put you on the spot like that."

She shook her head so hard that her curls bounced. "No. It's okay. I mean, you're right. I should have written to you." Shoulders drooping, she sighed. "I did write you."

His forehead wrinkled, and he rubbed at it, trying to remember if he'd forgotten mail from her. No. He'd remember that. He'd have cherished anything from her. It would have been worn thin from refolding, rereading. And he didn't have anything like that.

"Only I never sent them."

That explained it.

Actually, no.

It didn't explain anything.

"I don't understand."

Her cheeks took on the color of a ripe strawberry before she buried her face in her hands. "I wrote to you every time you wrote to me. But I chickened out before mailing them." She peeked between her fingers, and he'd never seen her look quite so vulnerable. Quite so adorable.

Setting his laptop and his search aside, he turned to face her. "I'm going to need a little more detail than that." His tone more resembled an interrogation than a man speaking to his wife, so he quickly adjusted it. "Didn't I say that I looked forward to hearing from you?"

"You did."

It was clear she wasn't going to continue and clear she couldn't meet his gaze, so he gave her jean-clad knee a nudge with his own. "So why not send them?"

Her eyes rolled toward the ceiling, holding on a spot above his head as she chewed on her thumbnail. When she opened her mouth, the words rolled out like a song. "They're kind of raw. *I* was raw. I was scared about Cody. I was starting over in a new city. At first, I didn't have any friends. Not to mention, I was married to a man I wasn't sure I knew."

That hit him like a punch to the jaw, ringing in his ears and drowning out what followed.

After a while her soliloquy died down, and she lowered her gaze to meet his. Her chin quivered as she admitted the most painful truth. "I wasn't sure I could trust you."

"And now?"

He held his breath, praying that she'd changed her mind about him, praying that he'd somehow proven that he was worthy of her trust. *Lord, I'd take another bullet to show her that she can rely on me.*

Despite the tremble still on display, she managed a half smile. She picked up his hand and pressed it over her heart. The beats were sure and steady.

"We wouldn't have survived the last weeks without you. There's no way." Tears pooled in her eyes, but she didn't look away. And she didn't blink them free. "I owe you my life. And my son's life. I'd trust you with anything."

Except her heart.

She didn't have to say it for him to hear it.

But for a moment he didn't care. Her trust was enough—even if he never had her love.

As one tear broke loose from her eyes, leaving a silver track down her cheek, he thumbed it away. Her skin was softer than a cloud, and she shivered at his touch. Leaning in, she pressed her hand to the middle of his chest, effectively stealing all of his air.

Fine with him. He didn't need it anyway.

"Thank you," she whispered, narrowing the gap between them.

"For what?" He sounded like a toad had taken up residence in his throat.

She sounded like a butterfly carried her words. "For being trustworthy."

And then she was a breath away. She closed her eyes, and her tongue darted across her lip. She fisted her fingers into his shirt and pulled him closer until there was only air and a prayer between them.

He was a goner.

There was no audience this time. No mistletoe. No coercion.

No surprise.

Still, when her lips met his, it felt like a boot to his stomach.

But a good one. The best one.

She was soft and yielding, yet she knew exactly what she wanted. And he was happy to give it.

Wrapping his arm around her waist, he pulled her to him. At first, she squeaked, startled, but then she sighed into him. She fit perfectly, like no one else ever had. Like they'd been made to connect like this.

Her fingers brushed around his ears and then latched behind his neck, holding him in place. It shot lightning through his mind until he couldn't remember why this was a bad idea. He couldn't think about anything except Kristi.

There was no room for regrets or might-have-beens.

He could only focus on keeping her right where she was for as long as she'd stay there. There was only her sweetness. Only her honesty. Only the way she made him want to be the best version of himself.

She needed that of him now. Second best wouldn't suffice for this operation.

Her shoulder brushed his, setting off another round of lightning. Sliding a hand into her hair, he combed his fingers through the curls. A callus on his palm snagged on a strand, tugging gently on her head. He froze, praying it wouldn't break the trance that encompassed them. He needed just another minute. If this was the last time he ever got to hold her this close, the last time he was ever surrounded by her sweet honeysuckle scent, he wanted it to be perfect.

And it was.

Her fingers tiptoed their way down the back of his neck, and he melted.

He lost track of who was holding whom. Arms entwined, hips and noses bumping, it didn't matter. Only that they were together.

And in another world maybe they could be together forever.

When she pulled away, her chest rose and fell in quick succession. His did, too.

Her fingertips were a whisper against his cheek. His eyes stayed closed, savoring the sensation, as she said, "I think I was a little bit scared of you."

This gut punch wasn't nearly as pleasant as the last. His eyes flew open. "You were afraid of me?" He hated the thought. Had he said something wrong or come on too strong?

"Not *you* exactly." She blinked bashful eyes open. "It was what you represented. A future I couldn't define."

He couldn't delineate their future either. Nothing was certain between them. He'd said they'd figure it out. But this was the first time they'd so much as broached the subject since their wedding day. And he didn't have any answers. Probably wouldn't for the foreseeable future. He couldn't possibly let her go until Cody was safe and the proud owner of a healthy heart. But then, once he knew that Kristi and Cody were free of danger and had a secure future ahead of them, did he really have the right to hold on to them? At that point, if she wanted to be free, he was honor bound to let her go.

But he couldn't worry about that for now. Not with the current problem requiring all his thought and concentration. He'd find that rich donor with a reason to need a heart—since apparently the scum didn't have one of his own. And then Zach would track him down and make sure he never hurt another child again.

TWELVE

Kristi could slap herself for waking up a second time regretting a kiss with Zach that never should have happened.

And yet the way he had held her so tenderly yet protectively and kissed her until she thought the top of her head might fly off had been more than she'd dare dream she'd ever experience again.

She hadn't once thought about Aaron.

At least not in the middle of it.

After? Well, that had been harder. After, she'd thought about her first and second kiss with Aaron. After, she couldn't help but compare. She'd also found herself wondering what he would think of all of this. Would he want her to be happy again?

But that was a ridiculous question. Aaron had sacrificed himself daily to make her happy, serving her in all the small ways. He made the bed every morning because he knew it was her least favorite chore. He put on a smiling face and ate her burnt casseroles every night that first year without complaint. He loved her.

Of course he wanted her to be happy—even if it meant moving on from him.

And he'd like knowing that his best friend was the

one who kept putting a smile on her face in the midst of such a terrible circumstance. So she didn't try to hide her smile as Zach barreled into the kitchen, his jaw covered in twenty-four hours of facial hair and eyes wild.

"I found it. I found him."

A band around her chest tightened as she searched for breath. "Who?" But she knew who. Only she didn't believe it could be real.

Zach plopped his laptop on the counter next to her bowl of oatmeal and pointed at the screen. "Look." He gasped for air, the first time she'd seen him so shaken up. Except for when he kissed her. But that was different. Sort of.

And there was no time to think about that.

She scanned the screen, which was filled with pictures of tuxedo-clad men and women in dazzling gowns. "What is this?"

"It's a pediatric heart disease fund-raiser. It was held in Palm Springs at one of the swanky resorts just a few months ago. See?" He pointed at a picture of a woman accepting a giant white check.

"But the donor we're looking for could be anyone."

He nodded, his hands moving a little too fast, his nostrils flaring. "I know. I looked up every name of every person identified at the event. And I dug up as much information as I could on each of them."

"When?"

"Last night. And this morning." He shrugged. "Had a hard time sleeping."

Heat rushed up her neck, but she forced herself to focus on the screen. "Anyone interesting?"

"A couple guys." He scrolled halfway down the event's page. "This one is the president of a bank. I don't know how much a guy like that makes. Maybe he doesn't have two million dollars to throw around, but it says here that he made a sizable donation to the foundation. If he doesn't usually have that kind of money on hand, he sure knows how to get it."

The man in question, D. Edward Baker, looked like her grandfather. Silver hair and bushy eyebrows did little to hide the sagging skin of his face. But his pale eyes were bright, and the corners wrinkled as he smiled.

He looked far too kind to be capable of targeting children, and she shook her head. "I don't think so."

Zach nodded but said, "We'll keep him on our list."

"Who else do you have?"

With a flip of his finger, the screen zipped down to another picture. This one of two men and a little girl. The girl was dressed up in her finest—a flowing gold gown and a tiara that cemented her position as a princess for the night. She held both men's hands, but only one had been caught by the camera smiling down at her. His bow tie was a little bit skewed, and despite the smile there was sadness in the lines around his mouth.

She pointed at him. "Who's that?"

Zach leaned over her shoulder, the impossibly soft cotton of his T-shirt brushing against her arm and his scent swirling around her until she felt a little light-headed.

"B. Loughlin. I looked him up, but there wasn't much info on him. He's in commercial real estate. But his buddy there, the one with the seventies mustache, is Carols del Olmo. That's the little girl's dad."

She squinted at the picture, a sizzle of recognition racing down her arms. "Do you know him?"

"No. Never seen him before in my life. Why? You?"

The memory was there, but she couldn't seem to put

her finger on it. "I'm not sure. I feel like I should know him. Like I've seen him before."

"Well, he does have quite a web presence, which isn't surprising since he's the CEO of a large tech company in Simi Valley. He's been in the news a few times talking about a federal lawsuit about tech security. Maybe that's where you've seen him?"

Kristi almost laughed. "I haven't watched the news in a year. There's no time between Cody and work and all of this."

"His company is worth nearly two billion dollars." Zach snorted. "And those are conservative estimates. The guy's loaded."

So the money wouldn't be an issue for him either.

But she couldn't shake the sense of his familiarity, and it bothered her. Was he a friend, or did he too closely resemble one of the guys who chased them at the mall? Or did he look like a celebrity she'd seen on the cover of a magazine in line at the grocery store?

He was rather handsome. His dark brown hair waved across his forehead, and his nose gave him a regal air. Even the mustache worked in his favor, making him look like a younger Tom Selleck.

Was that why he looked so familiar?

"Is he in any of the other pictures?"

With a shrug that said Zach didn't know, he scrolled down the page. The steady stream of pictures gave way to an article about the event, interspersed with an occasional picture here and there.

Suddenly one all but reached out and grabbed her. "Wait. Stop. Look."

Zach squinted and leaned in. It seemed to take a moment for the truth to register with him, but when it did, his mouth dropped open. "That's—"

"Denise Engle." Her stomach rebelled, and she wrapped her arms around herself. It didn't do much to help. "I saw that picture in Denise's office, too. She has it hanging on the wall next to her desk. I knew I'd seen him before."

"Are they… I don't know. Friends?"

"I have no idea. She's not returning my phone calls right now. Maybe he's the real reason she's not going to release the names on the transplant list." She scrolled back up to the picture of him and the little girl. "Do you think his daughter needs the heart?"

"I don't know. But I sure think a dad would do anything he could to save his child. It's worth asking him."

"Asking him? How are we going to track down a billionaire CEO?"

Zach worked his hand over his head a few times. "Well, I can probably find his address."

"You can?"

Zach shot her a you've-got-be-kidding-me look and gently pressed her out of the way so he could stand in front of the laptop. With a few clicks, he popped up a website that promised public addresses. But a search for Carlos del Olmo drew a blank. "No problem. County records are open to the public. If he owns property, it'll be on here."

Fingers flying over the keyboard, he worked his way into the county property records, searched and brought up five addresses in the Simi Valley area all belonging to Carlos del Olmo.

Her shoulders drooped, and the hope that had been building inside evaporated.

He laughed, and she gave him a pointed, but gentle, elbow to the stomach. "We don't have time to run around to all of these places," she reminded him.

His eyebrows danced. "No need. Let's take a look at these properties on a map. A man like del Olmo may own an apartment building, but you can be sure he's not living there."

A tiny smile crept across her lips. "How'd you get so smart?"

Shooting her a sly wink, he navigated to an aerial map that showed a view of the property. The first was very clearly a business. The building was large and blocky, and from the street level, they could see a sign. Del Olmo Technologies. His office building.

Her stomach sank, but she plastered a smile in place, encouraging him to try again.

The second address showed a large road in the middle of the desert that didn't seem to connect to anything except a metal barn of some sort.

"That's a runway. It's a private airport."

Her jaw dropped. "He owns that?"

"It sure looks that way."

If he owned his own runway and hangar, he almost certainly owned his own airplane. While the display of wealth was staggering, it managed to produce one thought on repeat.

Two million dollars had to be chump change to this man. Not to mention whatever he was paying the guys who had been following them and placing bombs in their home and car.

The next two addresses were additional office space, and by the last of the list, Kristi had reached for Zach's arm. Squeezing. Hoping. Praying that this last lead would let them find his home address. Let them find this man.

Zach hit a button, and a gray fortress appeared on the screen.

It was surrounded by twelve-foot security walls, and even from the overhead view, she could see the black cameras mounted at specific intervals around the property that guaranteed no blind spots.

Her mouth went dry, and her fingers dug into Zach's flesh. When she tried to speak, her tongue felt like it had doubled in size. Swallowing twice, she finally managed to loosen it up enough to utter her incredulous question. "How are we supposed to get in there?"

Zach's head was cocked to the side, his eyes narrowed and volleying back and forth across the screen. She could practically see his brain working out the hows. He wasn't the type to give up—she was sure he would find a way in.

She was just a little worried about getting out without ending up in handcuffs.

A man with that much security probably wasn't relying entirely on gadgets. Even if that was his specialty.

Nope. He'd have man power inside those walls.

And then where would they be?

"That's our way in." Zach pointed, but she wasn't following.

"Over the front gate?"

He chuckled. "Through it. Preferably when it's open."

She frowned. "But they'll know we're there."

"They're going to know either way. Best to announce ourselves and ask for an audience with the CEO."

"Couldn't you get in?"

He shot her a look like he couldn't believe she even had to ask. "Of course I could. There." He pointed to a corner of the outer wall. "And there. And there, too."

"But you still want to go through the front gate?"

"What I want is for us to stick together. And for neither of us to be arrested. And preferably for neither of us to get shot. Again."

She cringed and shot a glance at his shoulder. "I'm sorry you were hit."

He smiled. "Don't be. It barely even itches anymore. All healed up. Besides." He held her gaze for a long second in a way that made her insides take a painful flip. "Better me than either of you."

There were no words to respond to that, so she nodded slowly.

"Simi Valley is only a couple hours away. You up for a little drive?"

She nodded again but shot a gaze up the stairs toward Cody's room, where the little boy was still sleeping. Taking him with them had been fine when they were going to Denise's office and to the Gammers'—people she had had no reason to believe wanted to hurt him. But to take him to the house of the man who might be trying to kill him? No. She couldn't.

Zach didn't need to ask what she meant. "I'll call Luke."

When they reached the front gate of the del Olmo estate, Zach was more than grateful that he'd made the decision not to try for an uninvited entry. Maybe the satellite picture online was outdated. Or maybe the angles had been wrong. But the front gate wasn't just a gate. It had a guardhouse.

Complete with an armed guard.

Not that he couldn't take the guy, if he had to. But it was clear from the way he put his hand on his holster as they drove up that the kid wasn't used to carrying a gun. Which meant he wasn't used to firing it.

Which meant Zach's or Kristi's chances of being accidentally shot rose exponentially.

God, give me the words to talk our way in. And out.

His gaze jumped to Kristi. He should have left her behind. Not that she'd have let him. Still. This could be trouble. Especially if the conversation got sticky inside.

If del Olmo was indeed the man behind these attacks, he wasn't afraid of a little collateral damage. And that's what Kristi and Zach would be.

If they didn't go about this the right way, they could end up in a world of trouble. If del Olmo got hostile with them, then the best-case scenario was that they'd end up in a jail cell for the foreseeable future, with Cody on his own.

Well, not quite. Luke and Mandy were with Cody, and they wouldn't leave him alone. Jordan knew what was going on, too. They'd step in. They'd protect him. After all, he was family. SEALs protected their family.

But he didn't want his brothers protecting his family. He wanted to be there to do it. He wanted to be the one to tuck Cody in at night and the one to hold Kristi's hand. And brush her hair out of her face. And kiss her cherry-red lips.

Focus on del Olmo, McCloud.

The billionaire was their only hope for answers. Zach didn't know where else to go. He'd exhausted every lead. Even if the CEO wasn't the man behind the attacks, he might be able to point them to the person who was. Especially if it was someone else at that benefit.

Twenty yards from the guardhouse, he slowed the car to a crawl. "There was a mall about ten miles back. If I dropped you off there, would you wait for me?"

Her lips pursed in indignation. "Why would I do that? I'm going with you."

"What if this is more dangerous than we accounted for?"

He wasn't worried about facing whatever threat came to himself. He could handle whatever was inside those walls.

But he wasn't sure Kristi could.

She squinted from him to the iron gates that loomed ahead then back. "I'll go wherever you go."

The absolute certainty in her words forced a smile he hadn't expected. But he quickly shoved it away. He debated playing the Cody card. If she thought for a minute that she'd be leaving Cody alone, she'd let him turn around.

But then what?

Then they'd be separated, and if he couldn't get back to her, she'd be alone and scared.

There weren't any good options.

His training said to never leave a man behind and never go in alone. Decision made. "All right. We'll go together." And then, just in case. "But do me a favor?"

"What kind of favor?"

"The kind that keeps us both alive."

Her jaw dropped, and he took quick advantage of her silence.

"We might have to do some fast talking. If this is our guy, he's tried to kill both of us before. I doubt he'd hesitate to do it again."

He could see the truth register in her eyes. It would be so easy to reach for her hand, to assure her that nothing like that was going to happen. That they'd be safe since del Olmo might not be their guy. But Zach couldn't say that while hoping the billionaire really was.

Because if he was the one responsible for the attacks, that meant Zach knew how to end this nightmare. Cody would be protected. Kristi wouldn't be in danger any longer.

His family would be safe.

"Here's the deal. We won't be safe if he thinks he can get rid of us without anyone realizing he's responsible. So we have to make sure that he believes that the police know where we are. We have to get him to believe that others suspect his involvement, too."

A coolness set into her eyes, but she nodded slowly. "Sure. Because he can't be officially questioned as the last person to see us alive. Not without putting everything he has at risk."

She was a fighter, a storm-the-castle, brandish-her-fists sort. Pride sizzled in his chest. "Exactly. How'd you know?"

The corner of her mouth worked its way up, despite what appeared to be her best efforts against it. The feisty smile that found its place hit him right between the ribs. "I've been reading legal thrillers since I was twelve. Think I haven't picked up a thing or two?"

Good girl.

As they reached the gate and the guardhouse—a stucco shanty on the wrong side of the fence—the guard, who was clearly a former jock who looked like he hadn't been able to give up the juice, leaned out of the stall. Pressing a hand against the door frame, he showed off the bulging veins in his forearms. His squint was hard but lacked any real depth. He was posturing for all his worth in a way that a true professional never would.

Zach frowned. He was less than impressed with this character.

"You have an appointment?" The guard's name badge said Nilsson, and his blond hair appeared to have received more care than any man's should.

"No."

"No one gets in without an appointment." Nilsson crossed those steroid-swelled arms over his chest and sniffed. His eyes darted in the direction they'd come from. A clear invitation to head back in it.

Zach nodded. "I think Mr. del Olmo will want to speak with me."

"You're wrong. Mr. del Olmo won't meet anyone without an appointment."

Sure. Right. That made sense. Only it wasn't going to keep Zach from talking to the man.

"Besides—" Nilsson huffed like he'd never met anyone as stupid as Zach "—he's not back yet."

Spine snapping straight, Zach nearly choked.

That had been easier than he expected. And a much better scenario than the ones that had been playing in his mind. If the man was due to return soon, then they could hopefully catch del Olmo when he arrived in his car—outside the house, without his entire security detail just a press of a button away.

He couldn't have planned it any better.

As long as they could get into position in time.

"Sorry to bother you then." Zach threw the car into Reverse, ignoring the frown and scrunched forehead of the guard. The kid stepped out of his shack in time to watch the car make a wild two-point turn, and Zach punched the gas.

"Where are we going?" Kristi's fingers dug into his arm on the console, but her neck never turned.

"The great thing about big estates in the hills like this—one entrance."

Her nose wrinkled like he was speaking a language she couldn't begin to understand.

"The guard said that del Olmo is out—but he's expected back. Soon."

"How do you know?" Kristi said.

Zach followed the curve of the road until the gray stucco walls and big house were no longer visible in his rearview mirror. "The guard was clear. 'He's not back *yet*.'" Laying heavily on the key word, he watched realization pass across her features.

"He's coming back. And this is the only way in." The singsong in her tone suggested she was incredibly proud of herself for putting the puzzle together.

He hated to dash her moment, so he bit back the whole truth. This was the only way in—by land. It wasn't unheard of for a wealthy businessman to have his own helicopter. After all, he had his own airport. But it was at least three miles away as the crow flies. So their best hope was that del Olmo had flown in on his private jet and had his driver pick him up there.

If not, they were back to square one to get inside those gates.

Besides, they had a bigger problem.

Getting del Olmo's car to stop wouldn't be as easy as flagging him down. A man so concerned with his personal security wouldn't stop on a deserted road just because a stranger waved.

Zach eyed the winding road ahead of them. It wasn't particularly wide. He could easily block it with his own car.

Except the shoulder on each side was plenty wide to accommodate a car that wanted to dodge around them. The desert sand stretched for about a dozen yards in each direction. The loose terrain might slow a town car down. But it wasn't going to stop it. And seeing Zach's car stopped in the middle of the road would put the other driver on high alert and make him even more determined to keep moving.

He sucked on his front teeth for a long second as he pulled up along the shoulder. Gazing up and down the road, he sighed. Without any intel about del Olmo's ETA, he could end up falling flat on his face.

But as far as he could see, his best—maybe his only—chance of bringing the other car to a stop might prove to be a little risky.

"You're thinking about doing something stupid. Aren't you?"

Zach jumped at Kristi's quiet question. Sometimes she could read him better than he wanted to admit.

But she wasn't wrong. Not that he was going to let that stop him.

Stupid covered a broad spectrum, and in the grand scheme of protecting Kristi and Cody, he was willing to go to either end of it.

So instead of confirming her suspicions, he smiled broadly. "It'll be fine." He wished he was as wholly certain as he sounded, so he shot a silent prayer heavenward.

Oh, God. Please protect us. If there's another way, please show me. Whatever happens, be with Kristi.

He wasn't scared of what might happen to him. But as he ran his fingers over her wild curls, his heart squeezed. She dipped her head, nuzzling his palm, and he forgot to breathe. There wasn't room in him to care about her and worry about himself. She filled every inch of his chest, and when she blinked her big eyes at him, the truth hit him like a sucker punch.

No matter how many times he'd told himself not to let himself love her, he'd gone and done it.

He'd fallen.

From twenty thousand feet.

Without a parachute.

Man, he was an idiot.

But there was no time to dissect that terrible fact.

Not when a faint cloud of dust appeared on the horizon.

"We're about to have company."

Kristi's eyes snapped forward, her fists pressed into her legs, arms trembling under the pressure. "How are we going to stop them?"

Pinching the bridge of his nose, he tried to come up with another idea. Anything else. But there wasn't time. This was his chance—his *only* chance—to get del Olmo to answer their questions.

"I have an idea." Without taking time to explain, he crawled out of the car and slammed the door behind him.

Before he was fully standing, Kristi wrenched open her own door and raced around the hood. "What is it?"

He cringed and tried not to look into her face. She'd already pegged his idea as a stupid one. And if he wasn't careful, she'd try to stop him.

Which wasn't an acceptable outcome.

Adrenaline kicked through his veins until his skin felt like it was two sizes too small. He cocked his head from side to side, popping his neck and trying to loosen his muscles. Loose was good. Loose kept him on his feet.

Tight could spell an injury he could ill afford.

The cloud on the horizon continued to grow, cutting the distance between them until he couldn't tell if the silver flash was a car or a sun-induced mirage.

"Zach?" She grabbed his hand and clung to it with

both of hers as the outline of the car became clearly visible. It was gunmetal silver, not black, as he'd expected.

But the sleek lines and glittering paint spoke one word louder than all the others.

Money.

Maybe del Olmo didn't have a driver. Maybe he liked zipping around under the clear blue California sky in a car that cost more than Zach could make in ten years.

Zach prayed he didn't damage it.

Spinning back toward her, he combed Kristi's hair behind her ear. "Stay put, no matter what—all right?"

"All right, but—"

He cut her off with a quick kiss to her cheek. Reassurance. And, if he was really honest with himself, a sweet connection that he craved. "This is going to look a lot worse than it is."

Then he turned and ran into the road.

THIRTEEN

Kristi grabbed for Zach's hand. "Wait. What?" What was going to look worse than it really was?

But it was too late. He was gone. Jumping in front of the flashy gray car.

"Zach!" Her cry died on her lips as he crashed onto the hood of the sports car, a solid thump echoing down the deserted road. It reverberated in her chest, stealing her breath and sucking the life out of her as surely as if she'd been the one hit.

Tires squealed. Someone yelled. She thought it might have been her.

She imagined she could hear the agony in Zach's scream. It twisted her stomach and punched hole after hole in her chest.

She tried to cry out again, but there was nothing behind it, no air within her to carry the scream past her lips.

And even though he'd told her to stay put, she was running toward him as fast as her stumbling steps would carry her.

Zach bounced off the car above one of the ornate headlights and disappeared on the far side just as the driver brought the car to a stop.

This was his plan? His stupid, ridiculous plan? Didn't he know that she'd do anything to save Cody, but she couldn't lose Zach in the process?

Asinine. Idiotic.

The list could go on and on but ended with one question.

What had he been thinking?

The driver's side door flew open, and a large man in jeans and a button-up shirt jumped out. "Hey! Are you okay?" The mustachioed man looked exactly as he had in his pictures—save for the casual attire. But she'd have recognized Carlos del Olmo anywhere, even as he squatted down in front of the car.

A long, low moan came from the vicinity of the passenger-side wheel, and Kristi hadn't heard anything so sweet since her son's first cries.

As soon as she knelt by Zach's head, Carlos jumped to his feet and backed away, his hand immediately reaching for the phone sticking out of his shirt pocket.

Zach was covered in dust, but his chest rose and fell in a steady, if rapid, motion. "What is wrong with you?" she said, the lump in her throat making it harder than usual to speak.

His forehead wrinkled, though he kept his eyes closed. "I had to get him to stop. Thought I could jump onto the hood, but he didn't slow down."

"I'll call an ambulance." Carlos held up his phone.

But before he could dial 911, Zach waved his hand. "I'll be all right. Kris-ti." His voice broke, and he cradled an arm around his ribs as he blinked several times into the bright sky. "Tell him. Ask him."

From her spot kneeling at Zach's head, she looked up into del Olmo's frowning face.

"You mean this wasn't an accident?" He gripped his

phone in front of him in a defensive move. "Who are you? What do you want?"

Her tongue suddenly felt heavy and listless, and the words she should say hid from her. "We're—I mean, I'm—my son... My son is Cody McCloud. Does that name mean anything to you?"

The billionaire frowned, looking bewildered. Did that mean he was innocent? Or did it mean that he hadn't even bothered to learn the names of the children he had his thugs targeting? Either way, he was holding his phone in front of him like he would call in his security team at any moment.

She was botching this. Bad. And she was shaking so hard from seeing Zach splayed on the ground that she couldn't wrangle her thoughts into anything resembling cohesion. Let alone anything compelling.

Then a hand found hers, Zach's thick fingers weaving between hers. His voice sounded like he'd just woken up, but his words were clear. "Ask about his daughter."

"My daughter?" Anger was starting to show through the bewilderment on his face. "I'm calling the cops."

She glanced at Zach, whose breathing had slowed to a much more natural pace. The tension that had pulled his skin so tight across his face had disappeared. He gave her a little shake of his head. He didn't need help. Just a moment to collect himself.

"Please. Don't. Just hear me out." She licked her parched lips and prayed for the right words to come. "My son is sick—he needs a heart transplant. He's been on the donor list for over a year now, and he's near the top. Is your daughter on the list, too?"

Carlos's dark eyebrows met over his nose. "My daughter's perfectly healthy. I'm sorry about your son, but I don't understand what your situation has to do with me. I don't personally handle my company's charitable giving. You can contact—"

"No. We don't want your money." The words came out quickly, but all she could think about was that if he was telling the truth—and from the way he was acting, she was fairly sure he was—then his daughter was fine, and he didn't need the heart. And if he didn't need the heart, he hadn't been after them.

His phone dropped to his side, but the confusion on his face didn't abate. "Then what do you want?"

"We think someone is—" Oh, dear. It was terrible to think about but a hundred times harder to say aloud. Her throat closed around the words as though her body physically refused to let her say them.

Zach rolled to his side, then pushed himself to a sitting position with a soft groan, his arm always protecting his side. Then he made it to his feet and held out a hand to help her up before turning to address del Olmo so she didn't have to. "A little girl on the transplant list was killed a few weeks ago. And now there have been multiple attacks against our son."

Her stomach lurched. And not because of the terrible ache his words produced. Because of the words themselves.

Our son.

It made her cheeks flush and her heart swell. Could it be Zach truly considered Cody his own?

"I'm sorry to hear that, but I still don't understand. What does this have to do with me?"

Zach let out a sigh, and his shoulders slumped a little. "Yeah," he said. "I know this must seem crazy. But the truth is, we thought you might have been connected to the attacks."

Thankfully Carlos looked more surprised than offended.

"Why on earth would I—?"

"Whoever's behind these attacks against Cody has money—a lot of it. They've hired professionals to come after us, and they tried to bribe the family of the little girl, who was killed, to give up her place on the list. They offered two million dollars, so we were looking for someone with a lot of money who had an interest in pediatric heart disease. You attended a fund-raiser last summer, didn't you?"

He pressed his thumb and forefinger across his mustache, flattening it out with the measured movement. "Sure. In Palm Springs, right? My director of communications wanted me to donate some money. She says it looks good for the company. And my CFO likes the tax deductions. I didn't mind—it's good work. I'm happy we can help with all sorts of things—camps for kids in wheelchairs, food banks, homeless shelters."

Kristi filled in the last for him. "And pediatric heart disease research."

When Carlos nodded, she sagged against Zach, who immediately wrapped his arm around her waist. She felt more than heard him suck in a sharp breath, and she moved to pull away from whatever injury he'd sustained in his ill-advised stunt. But the arm at her waist locked into place, and he didn't let her shift away. He seemed to know that everything she'd hoped for was crumbling at her feet, and he wasn't letting her stand to face it alone.

Del Olmo wasn't going to be any help. He had no particular interest in heart disease and no use for the heart that could have been Greta's. The one that might be Cody's.

"We saw the pictures from the benefit," Zach explained, "including one of you with your daughter. We thought she might need a transplant, also."

"And if she did," Carlos continued, putting the pieces together, "you thought I'd be willing to pay someone to take out other kids if they stood between her and the top of the transplant list."

Zach nodded slowly.

"That's… I don't even have words for what that is," Carlos said. "I hope you don't think that I—"

"We know," Kristi interrupted. "We believe you. We're just…really desperate to find answers." And now they were at another dead end.

"Listen, I really am sorry about your son. That's tough." Carlos shoved his hands in his pockets, his frown filled with genuine concern. "I don't have any idea who might be targeting him…but maybe I can help in another way? I have a friend who works with kids who need organs."

Zach's body immediately stiffened, a low vibration flowing out of every pore. "A friend?"

"She's a transplant coordinator."

Kristi chomped on her tongue to keep from filling in the name she somehow already knew he would say.

"Denise Engle."

Kristi let out a sigh, but Zach didn't even pause. Instead, he jumped in with questions she hadn't even begun to formulate. "How do you know her? Is she the reason you were at the party or chose that foundation?"

Carlos shrugged. "We went to high school together. I didn't even know she was going to be at the fund-raiser until I got there, but after I saw her, I remembered that my director of communications had told me that someone I knew had called, asking about the donation. I didn't know it was Denise, but it wasn't unusual. We'd stayed in touch through college and a little after. And when my first company was sold for seven million, old friends started coming out of the woodwork."

Kristi nodded in understanding, and Zach kept them moving forward. "And did she say or do anything strange?"

Those dark brown eyebrows met again. "Like what?"

Zach lifted a shoulder. "Like ask you if she could borrow some money. Or did she ask for your help with anything unusual?"

"No, no. Nothing like that. But..."

Kristi held her breath and squeezed a hand into Zach's waist to keep herself upright. Just long enough to hear what Carlos might say. What Denise had asked him for.

"She did ask me a cybersecurity question. It was a little unusual."

Shivers raced down her spine. Denise was involved in the attacks against Greta and Cody. Kristi was sure. She just didn't know how.

Carlos looked right into her face, but his eyes were focused on the past. "Very weird, actually. I thought about it for a few days after that conversation. We had bumped into each other when we came in, but we weren't seated at the same table. So after dinner, I got up to network, and she came up to me out of nowhere. One minute I had a clear path to see a former Stanford classmate. The next, Denise was dragging me around the side of a big fountain."

She could see the same look on Zach's face that must have been on hers—the urge to push him faster but the fear of missing a key part of the story.

"She made small talk for a second and then said

she had a question. For her cousin, she was careful to specify. She wanted to know if it was possible to make a secure server look like it had been hacked." His face mimicked the confusion he must have felt on the evening of the conversation. "I didn't understand. Still don't. It was clear she didn't know exactly what she was asking for. She was really confused."

That made two of them. Kristi had no idea what he was talking about.

Carlos crossed his arms and shook his head. "Honestly I thought she'd had a few too many drinks at the open bar, so I dismissed it and never followed up. You think it has something to do with your son?"

Kristi wasn't sure how this nugget of information fit into the big picture, but Zach nodded his head. "Sure do." He reached out his hand and shook Carlos's when it was offered. "Thank you for your time. I'm sorry about that." He glanced back at the hood of the car. "I didn't mean to hit you so hard."

Carlos chuckled. "I'm pretty sure I'm the one who hit *you*. I'm sorry I looked down for a second. By the time I saw you I didn't have time to slow all the way down. Hope you're not hurt. You sure you don't want me to call for an ambulance?"

By way of a quick squat and two arm windmills, Zach confirmed he was physically fit.

Maybe Carlos didn't see it, but Zach couldn't hide his wince from Kristi as his arm hit its apex the second time around.

Handing a card to Zach, Carlos nodded. "Sorry I couldn't be more help. If you need anything else, this has my private office number so you don't have to get through the front-gate guard. Or worse, my secretary."

The impromptu roadside party split up. Carlos got

in his car and flew off in the direction of his house as Zach and Kristi climbed into his car. But before they moved, Zach leaned over the console.

"Something is going on with Denise Engle."

"Yes. But I don't understand what she was asking about with the server."

If she'd expected Zach to sound frustrated, she was pleasantly surprised. "So a computer's server is the home where a slew of digital information is stored."

"The info's not on the computer itself?"

"For a personal computer, sure. But if you've got a big network—like a company or a large foundation— where a lot of computers all need to access a central base of information, you'd store it on a server."

"Okay."

"And if a hacker broke into that server, he could access any of the information on it. If you're a credit card company and someone hacked your server, they'd have access to the card numbers of your customers."

Sure. She'd heard of things like that happening. Her bank had sent her a new credit card a few months back because it thought some of her information might have been illegally accessed. "But what do credit cards have to do with Cody's heart?"

"The information on the server doesn't have to be financial."

It all slammed into place like a garage door with a broken chain. On track, but heavy and loud. "Like a list of the names of the children waiting for a transplant."

"Bingo."

"So you think someone hacked into the server?"

Zach scratched at his chin, his gaze wandering past her. "Not exactly. Carlos said that Denise said that she wanted to make it *look* like a server had been hacked.

She wanted to know how to create a trail that would *appear* like someone had gotten in. Maybe even if no one had."

"Because the information was leaked by someone who already had access to those names." Her stomach twisted. "And she wanted to cover it up by blaming an anonymous hacker."

"We've got to talk with Denise."

That was an understatement. Either Denise was responsible, or she was covering for someone who was. Either way, she knew a whole lot more than she had let on.

Anger boiled below her skin, and Kristi scowled—but she felt her anger give way immediately to concern as Zach let out a little hiss when he reached for and buckled his seat belt.

"Are you okay to drive?"

He narrowed his gaze on her, intense and knowing. It sent a bolt of lightning shooting through her chest. "How do you read me so well?"

Ignoring the effects of those hypnotizing eyes, she stared back at him with all the force she could muster. "Why do you always avoid answering my questions by asking another one?"

That made him chuckle, and he shoved the key in place, turned over the engine and began the trek down the hill. "I'm fine."

"Stop saying that."

Ugh. Her tone was so much sharper than she wanted it to be. He just didn't understand that she knew what it was like to lose the man she had loved. She didn't want to do it again. And Zach was—

Wait a minute, had she just thought of Zach as the man she loved?

Oh, Lord. Please, no.

But her prayer was too little too late. She should have been guarding her heart. Instead, it felt like she'd just stepped on it.

Rubbing at the ache in her chest, she hunched over in her seat. What was she thinking? Falling in love with her husband was the worst thing she could do.

Especially since he didn't love her back.

He never had, and he never would. He was taking care of her and Cody because he felt responsible for them. There was nothing more to it than that. Yet, he'd wormed his way beneath her skin and into her very soul. He'd made himself indispensable, the linchpin in her life she'd never even known she needed.

No. No. No.

A whole-body shiver crashed through her, as though she could shake off the truth.

It didn't work. There was a light in her chest that was just for him. It flickered like a candle in a Montana blizzard, but it refused to be extinguished. It refused to dim, refused to do anything but attest to the love that had thawed her heart.

After the pain of losing Aaron, she'd assumed she couldn't possibly fall in love again. But it had been two years, and this love—this strange light inside— had very little to do with Aaron and everything to do with the man sitting at her side. The one who cared for her and her son not like he had to, but like he wanted to. The one who seemed to know just when to reach for her hand. The one who continued to put himself in danger to save them.

She gasped at the memory that flashed across her mind's eye of Zach jumping onto the hood of the car.

He'd tumbled, and she'd been able to think only one thing. *This was so much worse than it looked.*

And then he went and proved her point. He reached for her hand and laced their fingers together. Like he intrinsically knew that she needed to feel his warmth and be reminded that he was safe and whole and not—hopefully—permanently injured.

Without looking away from the horizon, he said in a quiet voice, "Cracked rib and a bruised hamstring. I'll heal."

"Are you serious? You say that like it's nothing." Frustrated, she jerked away from his touch. Didn't he know that it was safe to open up to her? Didn't he trust her to take care of him like she trusted him? Didn't he care how she felt? "Why do you always have to be such a tough guy? Why can't you ever just decide to get it checked out? I mean, you refused to spend a night in the hospital when you got shot, for crying out loud. *Shot!*"

He was silent for a very long moment, and both of his hands gripped the steering wheel until his knuckles turned white.

She felt a stab of guilt for adding to his stress when he was already injured. "I'm sorry. It's just that I hate seeing you in pain. I hate that you keep putting yourself in danger." It was too familiar. Too much like the pregnant clerk whom Aaron had stepped in front of at that convenience store.

But could it be that that courage, that willingness to sacrifice his safety to protect someone else, had been one of the reasons she loved Aaron? One of the reasons it had been so easy to fall for Zach, too?

Still, could it hurt for him to show a touch of fear? He ran into every situation headfirst, his decisions instantaneous and always so certain. Maybe if he showed a touch of hesitancy or a moment of consideration, she could believe he was actually concerned about the risk of dying and leaving behind her and Cody.

"I'm sorry you feel that way." He ground the words. "But that's not going to change. That's not who I am. I'm not… I'm not that guy."

For a split second she thought maybe he'd been about to compare himself to Aaron. But why would he? Zach had never promised her a future or a real marriage or anything beyond Cody's surgery. Because he didn't want any of those things.

Did he?

The words dried up, so they sat in silence as the car bumped down the road, onto the interstate and most of the way home.

Thirty minutes away from the house, a shrill ring echoed through the car. It beeped and honked, and Zach swung his gaze on her. "Is that your phone?"

"No."

But his gaze dropped to her purse at her feet, and she recognized the noise was definitely coming from that direction. Grabbing her tote, she dug through all of the effects moms were required to carry. A packet of tissues, toys to distract little boys and bandages for scuffed knees. Finally her hand wrapped around her phone.

It was silent, its screen blank.

But the shrieking continued. And finally, realization struck. Her stomach dropped. Tears gushed into her eyes.

"It's not *my* phone. It's *the* phone." With blurry eyes, she fumbled to open the zipper to the secret pocket in her bag.

Wrinkles furrowed above his brow. "Which phone?"

"The one from the hospital."

The zipper finally gave way. There was no telling if the phone shook on its own or because of her trembling hands, but she pressed it to her ear anyway.

"Hello?"

"Kristi McCloud?"

"Yes. Do you have a heart?"

"Yes, ma'am. Please bring Cody to the hospital immediately. The organ is en route, and we'll prep him for surgery right away."

She looked at Zach, wishing he could read her mind. "We're close. We're a few minutes away."

"Twenty-five." His tone was that implacable, calm-and-controlled one that she'd just been lamenting about, and suddenly it was the most comforting sound in the world.

"We'll be there in twenty-five minutes."

"Yes, ma'am." The disembodied voice gave her several more instructions, which she carefully repeated so that Zach would know what to do. By the time she hung up, her whole body trembled, and her breaths were little more than silent sobs.

Her baby was going to get a heart. He would get his heart. And then he would be saved.

Saved from the disease that ravaged his body. Saved from every painful breath.

And saved from the madman who wanted that heart, too.

FOURTEEN

Kristi couldn't fully remember anything that happened during the next seven days. Everything after the moment they picked up Cody at home, snagged his prepacked bag and raced to the hospital was a blur. There were hours and hours spent either fidgeting in a hard waiting room chair or pacing the confines of the tiny space, trying not to disturb the other family in the far corner.

Her head spun and her chest ached, and no amount of aspirin could touch the vicious pounding over her ears.

Fear and sorrow seemed to mingle in equal parts and with equal strength. Fear for Cody's safety and recovery. Sorrow for a family, who, like Greta's parents, mourned the loss of a child.

In their wake they left only a numbness.

She tried to find joy or hope or even a sense of peace and fell flat. Except when Zach reached for her.

He was the one thing that stuck and soothed through it all. Holding her hand as she sat still. Whispering quiet prayers for Cody, for her. Wrapping his arms around her at the exact moment she was sure she would fly apart. Pressing his lips to her temples, as though he could kiss away her pain.

And maybe he could. Because having him nearby eased her fears enough to let her rest her head on his shoulder. To disappear into his embrace.

Almost seven hours after they reached the hospital, the doctor walked in, his face solemn, tired. But there was a glimmer of satisfaction in the line of his lips. "The new heart is beating on its own." Everything after that was lost to the rush of relief louder than a locomotive.

They'd gone from the waiting room to the ICU room. Cody's body had been dwarfed by the full-size bed covered in ugly brown blankets. She'd wanted to turn to Zach and beg him to go get Cody's Corvette blanket. But it wouldn't be allowed in intensive care, not when germs and infections were a very real threat.

The machines beeped; the ventilator whooshed. And Cody's chest rose and fell. Slowly color began to return to his lips and to the skin under his fingernails. At the same pace hope seeped through Kristi, replacing the shock.

The nurses came and checked the incision that ran from his throat to his belly button. They checked his vitals every hour, checked his color, checked his responses. And then they took out the tube that had been breathing for him. And Kristi held her own breath, praying he'd suck in the antiseptic-scented air.

He did.

She cried.

And the days flew by.

But always Zach was by her side, bringing her food, bringing her clothes from home, bringing her coffee before she could even ask for it. Bringing her prayers and peace.

The shadow that had kept her locked in fear for so long finally lifted.

Perhaps they weren't out of the woods yet. There would be years of medication and doctor's visits and watching for signs of organ rejection.

But all those were hurdles that came with the greatest gift of all. A new heart. The chance of a healthy life.

And so, on the day that Cody was being moved from the ICU to the standard pediatric unit, Kristi found her way to the hospital's small chapel. It was quiet and dimly lit, save for a handful of candles flickering near the altar.

Lowering herself into a chair, she rested folded hands on the back of the seat in front of her. Bowing her head and closing her eyes, she whispered the only thing she could think to say. "Thank You. Thank You for saving my son. Thank You for sending Zach. I didn't know how much I was going to need him. But You did, didn't You?"

She didn't expect an answer, so she jumped when the door behind her clicked.

The man she'd just been praying about stood in the doorway, and her throat closed up. She said another prayer—this one silent, so that he hadn't heard her words.

"Mind if I join you?"

She shook her head, and he slipped down the aisle like a shadow.

"Cody is resting right now. But the ICU nurse is with him, getting him ready to move rooms. She said she's going to miss her favorite patient."

Oh, and thank You for the nurses who have taken such good care of Cody.

Zach reached for her folded hands, then stopped and let his hand drop to his knee. She physically felt the absence of his touch, the coolness where his skin should have been warm against hers. "You haven't slept much this week," he said. "How are you holding up?"

Her head buzzed too hard to find an answer for him. And her skin itched, sleep the only prescription. Forcing her lips not to tremble, she said, "I'll be fine whenever Cody is."

"I wouldn't expect anything less. What can I do for you? Do you want food? Fresh clothes? A book or magazine?"

By candlelight his features softened. Gone were the hard edges of his jaw and the bold planes. They were replaced by shifting shadows.

And always a familiar tenderness.

The only thing she wanted from him in that moment was his touch.

"Hold me?"

Surprise registered on his face, and he held so still that she thought he might turn her down. But before she could wrap her arms around herself, he took care of it. He enfolded her, his scent whispering around her, replacing the sharp tang of the sterile hallways with warmth and spice. When he rested his cheek on top of her head, she could feel him smile. And she let go. All the tears she'd been holding back so tightly leaked down her cheeks.

He'd always known how to hold her—even when they were teenagers. And he'd never once teased her about needing it.

Because maybe—just maybe—he cared about her half as much as she loved him?

"We're going to be okay now, right?" she asked.

She hoped for an immediate, swift confirmation, but she didn't get it. Instead, he dragged out a sigh that seemed to say he wished it was so.

"We can't still be in danger from whoever was after us before." She tried to sound confident, only partially succeeding. "Can we?"

He shook his head against hers, conveying his concerns and hesitations through the simple motion. "I don't know. It feels too easy."

"Cody getting a heart?" It had been anything but easy. Zach should know. He'd been there for every hour of it.

"No. Not his heart."

She sighed.

"The part where the man who tried to kill us suddenly moves on to another family. Another child." His voice sounded like it had been dragged across gravel. "People are still in danger."

She knew that deep inside. But she didn't have the strength to acknowledge and face it. She barely had the strength to hold her head up after seven nights of sleeping in an uncomfortable chair at the bedside of her child.

Looking up at his cheek, she ran a finger across the stubble growing there. His skin quivered. Could her touch affect him so? And how would she be affected by him? She knew their kisses had been electric, but maybe it was the threat that surrounded them that made the connection so intense.

Now that they were safe, a tug deep in her stomach ached to know if her connection with Zach would remain. If kissing him now would be the same as it had been before.

Even more, this might be her last chance. What if he never held her like this again? Her future was as unsure as it had been fourteen months before.

Cody had been saved. But now she might lose Zach.

Big fingers ran through her hair, cupping the back of her head and tilting it upward.

Her gaze didn't make it any farther north than his lips. Both sides stretched into a full grin as he ran a thumb across her chin. Her insides danced as he closed the distance between them by half. But he stopped there, and she could do nothing but lean in toward him. Pressing a hand against his chest, she tried to steady herself— and utterly failed.

The tender skin on her face was nearly on fire from his touch, but she craved more. More that he didn't seem inclined to give.

Wrapping her hand into the cotton of his shirt, she pulled on him just enough to get him moving. Still, only his breath reached her face. It wasn't enough.

Please. Please.

She needed this connection at least one more time.

He remained like stone, unmoving. But far from cold. Far from uncaring.

The tender embrace around her waist made her heart pound. With each breath, they came more fully in contact, and her breath hitched. Every time.

And the thumb at her cheek traveled the damp trail of her tears until she turned into a puddle herself.

But he still didn't move.

Well, that didn't mean she couldn't.

Pushing herself up, she leaned in, pressing her lips to his. Hard. Insistent.

Finally he moved, cupping her face and tilting her head until their connection was sure and sweet. And so rich.

It zinged at the back of her throat like she'd eaten all the frosting off a cupcake.

The kiss was equal parts thrilling and settling. His

touch made her feel like she was a rocket about to explode. Yet she didn't want to be anywhere but in his arms.

When he sighed her name against her lips, she dared to hope that he might feel the same. But before she could begin to ask, someone in the back of the chapel cleared her throat.

Kristi ripped herself out of Zach's arms and spun to face Cody's nurse, Jessica.

"We're getting ready to move him. Want to help him get settled into his new room?"

Kristi glanced down at Zach, who was staring at her with narrowed eyes that were filled with questions. Ones she wanted to answer. But was now the right time?

"You go," he said. "I'll be right behind you."

She nodded and was halfway down the aisle before she remembered what this move would mean for Cody's comfort. "Zach, would you mind running home? Now that we don't have the ICU restrictions, I think Cody would like his blanket."

"Of course."

She followed Jessica down the hall, then walked beside the rolling hospital bed as they entered the elevator.

"How you feeling, little man?" Kristi pressed her hand to the bland hospital blanket covering Cody's legs.

He lay relatively still, having given up shrugging or motioning to express himself. She couldn't imagine how much his little body ached. Even his voice was pitiful. "Okay, I guess. When do I get to go home?"

Jessica chuckled. "Not quite yet. The doctor still wants to watch you for a little while longer. We need to make sure you're taking all of your medications at the right time and getting your strength up. Before you can leave, you'll have to show the doctor that you can walk all the way to the end of the hallway."

Cody's pink lips pinched to the side. "Which hallway? The little one?"

Jessica reached into the pocket of her scrubs and pulled out a pen before scribbling on his chart. "Ornery as ever, huh? I'm marking that down so the doctor knows just how sneaky you are."

Cody's smile was contagious, and Kristi laughed. "You're a good kid."

"I know, Mom."

They all laughed at that as Jessica steered them into a single room with a large blue curtain hanging from a track on the ceiling.

Something billowed behind the curtain, and Kristi's stomach dropped.

Was someone waiting for them?

No. They weren't in danger any longer. She had to remind herself that they were out from under that shroud.

Weren't they?

Cody had his heart. No one would try to steal it from him now.

He was no longer on the transplant list. He was a success story.

She swallowed the strange punch of anxiety and swished the curtain out of the way. The room was empty.

Of course it was.

"Are you all right?"

Kristi tried to smile at the nurse but came up severely short. "I think so."

Not looking fully convinced, Jessica turned back to Cody. "Hang tight. Let me get an extra set of hands to help me transfer you to the other bed."

"Sure." Cody closed his eyes as the rubber soles on Jessica's shoes squeaked their retreat.

But they weren't alone. Kristi could feel it.

She couldn't hear it. There was no loud breathing or audible movement. And she couldn't see it. But somehow, she knew that trouble was brewing. She could feel the weight of that invisible gaze—the same one she'd felt a hundred times and had thought was Jackson Cole.

Only now she knew he wasn't the one after her. And not knowing who was lurking in the shadows was so much worse.

She spun around and around, searching to find the source. No cameras. No signs of life. No one.

They were alone.

But they weren't.

As she reached to open the big wooden door, it flew in and slammed against her forehead.

She staggered back, tripping over her own feet and falling into the railing of Cody's bed.

"Momma?" His cry barely made it through the alarms clanging in her head, and she squinted into the familiar face of a man looming over her.

Kicking at his shin, she screamed.

He cut the sound off before it even began, pressing his hand over her mouth and his foot against her neck. She clawed and kicked at him, but none of it made a difference.

Cody cried, and she prayed it would be enough to garner the attention of someone passing by.

"Shut up or your mommy is going to get it."

She heard Cody's cries die down to whimpers. She thrashed against his hold, desperate to reach out and comfort her son. But her strength was disappearing. No matter how hard she gasped, there was no air to breathe.

The pressure on her neck increased, and everything in her cried for relief.

But her arms were limp, her legs useless.

As her vision narrowed, she saw another figure scoop up Cody just before everything went black.

FIFTEEN

Zach knew there was something wrong as soon as the elevator doors opened. The nurses station was a flurry of activity, and a uniformed security guard was waving his arms about as he talked with two police officers.

Zach clenched his hands into Cody's fuzzy blanket tighter and tighter until his arms shook and he could see only red.

He'd gone after the blanket and left them alone.

Because he'd foolishly thought they were safe. He'd wanted so badly to believe that the danger had passed and that there might be some hope for a future.

And he'd left them to what?

He had no idea what had happened, but he had to find out. Not knowing was so much worse than the horrors his mind could conjure.

He started running the moment his foot hit the slick white tile, and he dashed past the cops, barging into Cody's room.

"What are you doing?" the security guard yelled at his back. "This room is off-limits."

Zach took his first real breath as he slammed to a stop inside the empty room. There wasn't a body. No hints of blood. The only sign of a struggle was the front bed, which was pushed to an odd angle despite the clearly engaged locks on the wheels.

"Where are they?" He spun on the red-faced guard, whose bluster died on his lips.

"Wh-who?"

"Are you kidding me?" Zach roared, shaking the blanket like a weapon. "My *son* and my *wife*. Where are Cody and Kristi?"

The guard looked like he was about to cry, so he pointed over his shoulder at the policemen, like they'd somehow made Zach's family disappear.

Unacceptable.

"Did anyone see anything? A nurse? Security footage?"

"The—the camera on this lev-level is broken. No one saw anything."

Doubly unacceptable.

The bustle from outside the room continued, but Zach shut it out, zeroing in on the guard, who had apparently decided to cooperate. Which was the idiot's first—and only—good decision thus far.

Zach scrubbed at the top of his head. "How long have they been gone?"

"Twenty minutes."

The whole room spun. Twenty minutes. They'd been gone almost as long as he had. And he'd made it to their home and back.

They could be anywhere by now.

Forcing his hands to stop shaking, he twisted up the blanket, searching for anything to help him find them.

He *had* to find them. There was no other option.

"I need to see security footage from the other floors, especially the ICU." The man didn't move. "Now."

Again the guard had the gall to point to the officers. "Can't. Only the cops can see it."

Zach was ready to spit fire. Instead, he swallowed the bile building in the back of his throat and spun on his heel. Sailing to the stairwell, he flew down four flights and back into the parking lot before he consciously realized where he was going.

Denise Engle.

She knew something, and it was a whole lot more than she'd been letting on.

He broke several posted speed limits on the short drive to her office, but he didn't have time to care. Nothing was going to stop him. Not even the secretary at the front desk of the transplant offices, who had the nerve to try to hold him up.

"You can't go in there, sir."

"I'm going to see Denise Engle."

The little woman with big blond hair waved her finger at him. "She's in a meeting. You can't see her."

Seriously? He'd faced down an entire terrorist cell in Lybania. And this woman thought she'd stand between him and the only person who might be able to give him answers about his family?

He stepped around her, never quite touching her, but showing her just what he was capable of doing. He wouldn't hurt her, but he wouldn't hesitate to restrain her.

Looking afraid, she tripped away from him, and he gave her a simple nod, affirming that she'd made the right choice.

Denise's name hung on a black plaque on the outside of her door. He didn't bother knocking or even pausing. He barely refrained from kicking down the door, just to vent some of his rage. Wrenching the handle and putting a shoulder into it, he crashed through.

Three stunned faces stared at him.

"I need a word," he said, ignoring the couple on the near side of the desk.

Denise stood, wiping flat palms down the sides of her skirt. "Would you give us a moment, please?"

The man and woman scurried out of the office like scared chipmunks.

Good. That's what he was going for. Intimidating. Daunting. Fire-breathing.

Maybe that was everything Kristi didn't want. But right now it was what she needed. And it was what he knew how to do.

Taking a deep breath through his nose, he let it out in a harsh burst. "Cody and Kristi have been taken. I think you know who is responsible."

She opened her mouth, looking like she was about to protest, but he cut her off with a wave of his hand. "Don't bother to deny it. They're gone. You're going to help me find them. I want. My wife. And son."

Tears sprang to her eyes, but he didn't have any sympathy for them. He couldn't feel anything but the acute loss of his family, the hole where they should have been.

"Tell me everything you know."

"I don't know anything." But her voice shook, and she immediately labeled herself a liar. "I don't know much."

Fear and anger warred inside him, battling for an outlet. But yelling and punching a wall wouldn't bring Kristi and Cody back.

God, give me strength. Give me courage. Show me what to do.

He'd done everything he knew to keep them safe. But

it hadn't been enough. Was this just another reminder that he wasn't the one for Kristi? That he couldn't be the one she needed? Or was this his opportunity to show her he could be there for her?

He had no answers.

Clenching shaking fists to his stomach, he narrowed his eyes and leaned in closer to Denise. He managed to keep his voice low but his meaning unmistakable.

"Start at the beginning."

Tears gushed down her cheeks, her eyes and the tip of her nose turning red. "I didn't mean to. I didn't know why he wanted the list."

"Who?"

"Loughlin. Bernard Loughlin."

"Who's that?" But his mind was already running through the list of names of the donors at the Palm Springs benefit. B. Loughlin. He'd been in the picture with del Olmo.

She hiccupped, and he invaded her space even more until she spilled like a fire hydrant. "He's a real estate mogul in Beverly Hills. He offered me half a million dollars for the list of transplant patients. Of course, I turned him down."

"Of course," Zach muttered under his breath.

"I said I couldn't," she protested. "But…"

"But?"

She caved. "But then he offered me a full million. And he threatened to have the bank foreclose on my mom's house if I didn't cooperate. She was behind on payments, and they were sending her notices, so I gave him the first name on the list."

"Greta Gammer."

She nodded, wiping her hands over her eyes and sniffling hard.

He could drum up no sympathy for her. "And then?"

"And then, after what happened to her, he said if I didn't give him the next names, he'd tell my supervisor what I'd done. And I would never work again. I could be convicted and sentenced to federal prison. Don't you see? I had to tell him."

"You gave him my son's name." He seethed the words through clenched teeth, everything inside him demanding that he make her see just what she'd done. Cody needed to be under a doctor's care, and every second he was out of the hospital increased the chance that he wouldn't make it back alive.

Unacceptable.

"Why? Why is he killing the kids on the donor list?"

"His son needs a new heart. But he has additional complications that make him less than an ideal recipient." She bit into her lips until they disappeared. "Most likely he'll never make it to the top of the list."

"Unless everyone in front of him dies first."

"Yes." It was more sob than actual word. "I'm so sorry. I didn't know what he would do. I thought he would try to buy the parents off."

"Oh, he did." The image of the Gammers' broken faces flashed before him. "But when he realized that everyone else loves their kids as much as he does, he went off script."

Zach leaned back and covered his face with his hands. "Why did he take Cody now, after the surgery?"

She choked on another sob. "His son is getting worse. And—and this is just a guess. But I think he wants that heart."

Zach squinted at her, trying to understand what he'd just heard. Surely no one could be that depraved. He'd seen the very worst in the world—but he couldn't fathom the idea of a man kidnapping and killing a little boy to steal his heart.

"Could a heart even survive a second transplant?"

She lifted one trembling shoulder. "No one's ever tried, as far as I know. But I doubt it. A heart is a muscle, and it needs time to recover after the trauma of transplant. I don't think it would work. But his son is running out of time—he doesn't have long enough to wait for another suitable donor."

"If he's planning to perform another surgery, he'd have to keep Cody alive, right? Long enough to get a doctor and operating room in place?"

"Yes."

The knot in his chest loosened just enough for him to catch his breath.

Cody could still be alive.

Zach prayed that Kristi was, too.

"Where are they?"

"I don't know."

"Denise, you're going to go to jail for selling the names and for your part in that little girl's death. You can't change that, but maybe you can save two other lives. And maybe the DA will look kindly on that."

Fear pulled her features tight across her face, her mouth nothing but a white line, her chin quivering. "I told you he's in real estate—he must have access to lots of properties! But..." she added, clearly thinking out loud. "If he was looking to hide out, he'd want somewhere secluded. He said something once about a cabin. In the woods. He mentioned there wasn't cell service there. That's all I know. I swear."

It wasn't much. But it was everything he had. He ran from the room, already punching his phone to call Jordan.

"You in trouble again, Ziggy?"

Zach didn't have time for Jordan's teasing, so he bypassed the joke and got straight to the real trouble. "Kristi and Cody have been kidnapped. I need you to find me a remote cabin owned by a man named Bernard Loughlin who lives in Beverly Hills."

His feet pounded on the tile flooring as he burst into the open. But the fresh air didn't slow his breathing or the painful thudding in his chest. He had to get to his car and find that cabin.

Jordan, like the brother he was, didn't ask any questions. He simply began typing, his fingers pounding on the keyboard on the other end of the call. "Loughlin. Bernard."

"Yes."

"Just a second. You said Beverly Hills?"

"Yes. But it might be in San Diego or Orange County." There weren't many spots without cell service anywhere in Southern California, but it didn't make sense to go any farther with a kid who needed constant medical attention.

Zach reached for the handle of his car door, only to realize he was still carrying Cody's blanket. Chucking it in the passenger seat, he slid into the car and drummed on the steering wheel. "Come on, Jordan. What have you got?"

"He owns a bunch of property, but it's mostly commercial."

Zach wanted to cry and scream. He settled for slamming his fist against the wheel. He didn't have time to lose.

He couldn't lose.

He couldn't lose Cody. Or Kristi. Or their silly dirty dishes in his sink.

He couldn't lose car shows on the TV or sweet smiles over a bowl of cereal.

He needed them.

"Got it. Fishing cabin on Lake Cuyamaca near Julian. It's about an hour outside town."

"Text me the address?"

"Done."

Zach hung up without the normal niceties. Jordan would understand. It was time to go get them. But he couldn't go in alone. Calling on his hands-free unit, Zach tried to reach Detective Sunny Diaz while he sailed out of the parking lot and toward the interstate.

"This is Diaz."

"Zach McCloud here. My wife and son were just kidnapped, but I know who took them and I have a pretty good idea where he went."

Kristi banged her head against something hard, but she couldn't tell if the resulting ringing was from the metal or inside her head. Everything ached, especially her throat, and she reached to massage it, only to find her wrists bound together in front of her.

Her surroundings rocked, and she crashed against the wall again. This time, she realized she was in a moving vehicle. If the cavernous bay was any indication, it was a stripped-down van. And if she had to take a shot, she'd guess it was black.

The interior was dim at best, the windows painted over. There was only a sliver of light through a crack where the double doors didn't quite meet. The light fell on a hospital-issue brown sock.

Fear seized her, and she threw herself forward, wrapping both hands around the sock and fighting tears when she realized there was a foot inside it.

She tiptoed her fingers up Cody's leg, to his hand and beyond. Careful not to bump the sutures that held him together where they'd spread his ribs, she found his neck and his cheeks and his ruffled hair.

He was warm and breathing.

She couldn't contain a quiet sob—a mingling of relief and terror.

Someone had taken her son. Stolen him when he most needed to be under a doctor's care. But at least he was still alive.

"Cody? Cody, buddy?"

"Momma?" His voice was little more than a breath, but she'd accept it and be grateful for it.

"Bud, are you hurt?"

"I can't see."

She found his arm and squeezed it. "I know. It's dark in here. But we'll stop soon."

"Where are we going?"

If only she knew. If only she could tell someone where to find them. How to save them. "I don't know. But we're together." Her voice cracked, and she fought the urge to curl into his side as he lay on some sort of makeshift mat.

"It'll be okay," he said.

"I know." But she was lying. She knew no such thing.

"Zach is going to come get us," her son assured her.

Zach.

His name rang through her mind over and over. A silent prayer for deliverance from whatever madman had taken them. *God, send Zach to save us. Before it's too late.*

They were on a clock. Cody had to have his medications at regular intervals, on time and always in the right dosages. His body required help to accept the alien organ. Without it he'd be lost.

The trouble was, she had no idea how much time had passed since he'd had his last dose.

Not that she had any medication to give him anyway.

This was not how it was supposed to work out. She'd prayed that Cody would be saved. She'd waited for a heart to become available. She'd done everything she could to protect him.

And now this.

This unknowing. This fear. This utter and literal darkness.

How could this be the end for them both?

And it would be. She wasn't foolish enough to think that they'd have any use for her after Cody was gone. And he would be gone if help didn't come.

Lord, please. Please. Send help.

Squeezing her eyes shut against the tears that pooled there, she leaned against the cold metal of the van's wall and imagined Zach's face. The warmth in his eyes and the tenderness in his smile filled her. The fervor of his last kiss still fresh on her lips battled the chill that seeped through her lightweight T-shirt.

She might never see him again. In fact, it was a strong likelihood that their last kiss had been their last ever.

Regret consumed her. She could have taken any of a dozen opportunities to tell him that she loved him. She should have found the words to tell him how much she wanted what they had on paper to be as real as the feelings in her heart.

Could-haves and should-haves.

Useless.

And utterly painful.

She slumped against the unforgiving floor just as they hit a pothole. It jarred her shoulder, and she cried out, a pathetic mewl at best.

"Momma?"

"Yeah, bud?"

His voice got softer, more childlike. "Don't worry. Zach is coming. He promised he'd take care of us, and he does what he says."

"Yeah. He'll be here soon."

She spoke the words because she wanted them to be true. But the flicker of doubt that had been inside her since Aaron had failed to come home fought for control. Maybe he wouldn't come. Not because he didn't want to but because he couldn't find them.

But her son's words rang through her. His faith was so sure. So certain. He didn't doubt Zach's arrival. Because he didn't doubt Zach.

Maybe that was why she'd failed to tell her husband what was in her heart.

She doubted he'd come back.

In that moment Cody was sure enough for the both of them. There was no hesitancy in his tone or stutter in his words. He trusted Zach. And she did, too. But whether he would find them in time to save them remained the question.

So she was going to have to keep them alive until then.

The thought shot through her like a forest fire. Zach would come. He'd promised. It was her job to make sure that they were alive when he got there.

The van's wheels squealed as it lumbered to a stop. A car door slammed. Scurrying toward the rear doors, she lay on her back and lifted her feet. When the door opened, if she could get enough force, she could slam it into their kidnapper. If she could knock him out or knock him off balance, maybe she'd be able to grab the keys and take the van back to the hospital.

She waited for the sound of the door unlocking. But there was nothing but footsteps growing fainter, like they were headed away from the van.

Minutes ticked by until her back ached and thighs cried from the awkward position. But the driver didn't return.

And then suddenly the side door was wrenched open with the clang of metal against metal. The setting sun flooded the interior, stinging her eyes, and she twisted away from it.

"Get the girl." The voice was high-pitched but not feminine. She didn't recognize it.

As the spots in front of her eyes stopped dancing, she focused on the speaker's face. Dark eyes and narrow features. She knew this man. At least she'd seen him before. In the pictures from the fund-raiser. He was the one they'd dismissed as not prominent enough.

But he was clearly crazy enough.

"I'll get the kid," he said to his cohort.

"Please, don't. He needs a doctor."

Cold, emotionless eyes turned toward her. "I have doctors on the way. He'll be fine. For now."

She crawled toward him. "Please. He's my son."

"I know. And you'll do exactly what I tell you or you'll watch him die."

The other man, who had stalked her in the mall and then attacked her at the hospital, grabbed her arm and jerked her free of the van. The angry sneer on his face was enough to tell her that it would be no use arguing with him either.

The shorter man—Loughlin, she was almost sure—

had pulled an EMT's gurney even with the van and slid Cody onto it. Leaning over her son, he smiled down at the boy like an uncle. A highly deranged one.

"How you feeling? How's your heart?"

"All right."

"Good. That's real good." He patted Cody's head like he was a puppy. "Now, listen close. You're going to do everything I say, okay?"

Cody looked toward her, and she tried to catch his gaze. "It'll be okay. I love you, little man!"

Loughlin raised his voice. "Everything I say. Understand? First, I want you to swallow this pill."

"A-and if I don't?" Cody managed to say. Kristi's heart twisted for her son, so clearly scared but still trying to be brave—to be like Zach.

"If you don't, I'll hurt your mom."

What kind of monster would say that to a child?

Cody whimpered, and Kristi fought to find her feet, but the guy from the mall pushed her back down.

"This is your immunosuppressant. You need this."

Kristi couldn't see the pill to confirm, but she prayed the man wasn't lying. If he wanted her son's heart, then he had to keep it safe and healthy inside Cody. She was counting on that. Praying it was the case. "It's okay, honey. Take the pill."

"That's a good boy. Now we wait for the doctor. This heart belongs to someone else."

SIXTEEN

Zach's car skidded to a stop about a hundred yards from the clearing where GPS promised he'd find Loughlin's cabin. He imagined he could make out the lights from the windows through the trees. Big green pines served as cover as he stepped out of his car. He'd made only one detour on the way out of town—to pick up his weapons.

He pulled on his shoulder holster, and he slid his six-inch knife inside its sheath in his boot.

When he stood up, he stretched his neck to each side before looking up at the sky. Night was closing in on them, the darkness all around a mirror to the blackness in the soul of the evil man in that cabin.

Kristi and Cody were being held, and he couldn't begin to imagine their fear. The man who had taken them was a lunatic. But Zach knew better than to underestimate him. Everything he'd done, from stalking Kristi to hiring a mercenary to blow up her car, had been cold and calculated. Which made him a very dangerous lunatic.

Bile rose in the back of his throat, and he had to lean his hands against the hood of his car to force it down. He had to get them out of there.

Detective Diaz had made him promise not to go in without her. "I'll call the local sheriff, and we'll get backup. Do not go in. You don't have any jurisdiction," she'd warned him.

Jurisdiction. That was the very least of his concerns at the moment.

Glancing at his watch, he squinted at the numbers. She should be here. She had lights and sirens working in her favor.

Zach just had a total disregard for posted speed limits.

Suddenly two bright headlights flew around a curve, and a sparkling new truck slid to a stop behind his car. Jordan jumped out before the engine had even fully stopped. Closing his door with a soft click, he spun to face Zach while he slid his weapon into place.

Zach couldn't hold back the grin that tugged at his mouth. "What are you doing here?" But he didn't really need to ask.

Jordan ignored the question and clapped him on the back. "What's the plan?"

"Loughlin has Kristi and Cody in the cabin. Just inside the clearing up the road."

"You have eyes on them?"

Fear and uncertainty spun in his middle, and he shook his head. "Not yet." There was no telling what he'd see when he did find them.

"You want me to check it out?"

Jordan seemed to know what Zach hadn't even acknowledged to himself. As soon as he got to the cabin, he wouldn't be able to wait a second longer before going in after them.

He was on the verge of suggesting they go in together when two more cars flew up the road. Gravel and dust filled the air as they skidded onto the shoulder, and a woman who had to be Sunny Diaz jumped out of her unmarked vehicle. She quickly introduced herself and then pointed to the sheriff's deputy in the brown uniform. "This is Lee Preston. He's with the San Diego County Sheriff's Office." Then she pointed at Zach. "This is Zach McCloud."

Zach nodded and hitched his head to his left. "Jordan Somerton."

Preston eyed both men with a hesitant gaze, especially when his gaze settled on their matching Sig Sauers. "You guys planning something?" He reached for his own weapon.

God bless Jordan Somerton. With all the nonchalance of a Girl Scout, he said, "I believe this is a rescue mission. That's a no-fail mission, if you're not familiar with it."

The skinny deputy's neck snapped to attention, and he scowled. "Detective Diaz and I will check out the cabin, and if there's anyone to rescue, I'll handle it."

"Negative." Again Jordan spoke when Zach's patience began to wane. "You're here for the arrest. We'll take care of the rest."

Preston sputtered at that, but Diaz nodded. "Let's work together and get this taken care of."

Zach took that as his cue to lead, and he set off through the trees. If he'd known the deputy would be so inept at stealth movement, he'd have told the kid to stay in his car. But with every step, he found a pinecone or twig to snap, each plucking his last nerve.

"Watch where you're stepping." Diaz kept her voice low but firm, and Zach had a flash of compassion for her, even though she hadn't been able to help them when Kristi had first asked.

Her warning seemed to help, and they approached the clearing in relative silence.

The single-story log cabin dominated the open space, stretching from tree line to tree line. A black van and an expensive foreign car were parked in clear view in the driveway. Lights shone from nearly every window of the house—an arrogant mistake.

Loughlin didn't think anyone would identify him or track him down.

He thought he'd gotten away with it.

He'd been wrong. And that arrogance wasn't doing him any favors.

Bright lights inside made it hard to see what was outside. And it made it a lot easier for those outside to see in.

Zach inched into the open, searching the exterior walls for motion-activated lights or alarms. There were none along the front porch. Just four main windows to the living room and a rocking chair that squeaked in the wind.

Jordan motioned to the right.

Zach nodded and motioned to the left.

The two men split, racing to opposite corners of the house. Jordan disappeared along the far wall. Zach reached the corner and turned just in time to see Diaz grab Preston by the collar to keep him from charging the front door and ruining any element of surprise.

He owed her some chocolate.

Dewy grass squished beneath his boots as he slipped to the lone window on this wall. It was low, about at his waist, so he ducked down before peeking inside.

His heart nearly stopped.

Cody lay on a paramedic's gurney on the right-hand

wall. His eyes were closed, and his chest didn't appear to be moving.

Tears flooded Zach's eyes, and he leaned his head back against the log exterior.

Too late. Too late.

The words rang like a mantra through his mind, the image of Cody's still form seared in his memory.

He risked another glance inside and let out a whoosh of air. Cody was rubbing his eyes and trying to sit up. He was alive. Not well. Not yet safe. But alive.

Suddenly Kristi appeared at Cody's side, stepping out of Zach's blind spot and standing between her son and the open door to the room. She cried loud and long, but her words were muffled by the window and the wall. Then he saw what had set her off.

Loughlin walked into the bedroom carrying a clear medical bag like those attached to IVs in the hospital. Except this wasn't a hospital. And whatever was in that bag wasn't for healing.

Kristi's scream rose, and this time he could make out her words. "Don't! Don't you dare!"

But Loughlin didn't stop. He charged forward, and when Kristi didn't move, he shoved her out of the way, the sound of her body hitting the floor echoing under the stars.

Fire raged through him, burning up everything he knew about conducting a mission.

First gather the intel. He had to know how many hostiles he was facing. What if there were three or four other guys inside? He could be walking into a trap. Rushing in would leave him unable to protect both Kristi and Cody.

It wasn't safe to go in yet. Not until he heard from Jordan that the rest of the house was clear.

But Loughlin wasn't on the same schedule. He hung the IV bag on the side of the bed and reached for Cody's arm. Kristi's hand clawed at his leg, but the man spun. Then he made a motion like he'd kicked a soccer ball.

Only it wasn't a ball.

It was Kristi.

Her scream tore him open, and he acted entirely on instinct. No way would he let them face Loughlin alone.

The window shattered with a sharp crash as he slammed through it, rolling onto the rough-hewn floorboards. He caught his injured shoulder on the corner of a short bookcase, but the pain didn't compare to the light that shone from Kristi's face. It was akin to relief, mixed with worry. And there was something else sprinkled over the top. Something he couldn't quite name that distracted him just long enough for Loughlin's backup to show up.

Rookie mistake on Zach's part. He could only hope the price for it wouldn't be too high.

The thug pulled out his 10 mm, and it fit into his hand like it had always been there. This wasn't a poseur like the guard at Carlos del Olmo's house, but a trained mercenary who knew what he was doing.

Zach crouched amid the shards of glass as Loughlin cried and dived toward Cody. "Not the boy."

But the thug wasn't pointing the gun at Cody or Kristi, who struggled to get up. The weapon was aimed directly at Zach, and at this range, the shooter wasn't going to miss.

Zach shot Kristi one more glance. She'd never be able to unsee what was about to happen. She'd never be able to see him as anything other than the warrior he was.

Which meant she'd never be able to see a future with him.

Springing from the floor, he launched himself across the room and slammed into the gunman. The thug grunted as Zach crashed against him and swung his hand at Zach's head. With his forearm, Zach blocked that punch but took another to the kidney. It stung like a hornet.

The man didn't fight fair, so Zach didn't either.

He grabbed the gun hand and twisted the barrel backward. At least two fingers snapped, and the man released his hold on the weapon, but he didn't stop fighting. Maybe he had nothing left to lose.

Zach blocked a scissor kick but took a boot to his knee. Pain shot up his leg and down to his toes, and he grunted into it but didn't let it drop him.

Kristi screamed, and Zach had had it with this place. A well-placed elbow to the sternum put the thug down hard, and he spun on Loughlin to find the madman cowering in front of Jordan's weapon where Zach's friend stood in the door.

"My son needs that heart. It should belong to him. It's his heart." Loughlin's crazy mutterings weren't helping his case. "It's mine. It's mine. I would have paid for it. I *tried* to pay for it. Those stupid people. They wouldn't take my money."

With the trouble eliminated, Detective Diaz and Deputy Preston entered to cuff Loughlin and the other man. The thug was sullenly mute as they read him his rights. But Loughlin never stopped talking.

Maybe watching a child dying would do that to a man. Make him lose his mind as surely as he was losing his son.

To an extent, Zach could understand. He was about to lose his whole family, and it was a pain unlike anything he'd ever imagined.

* * *

"You want to go home for Christmas?"

Kristi looked up at the doctor who'd spoken to her son. She could hardly believe the hopeful words, but the man was smiling as he looked over Cody's chart. His shaggy hair flopped around as he nodded.

"Well, all your stats look good, and Nurse Jennie told me you made it to the end of the hall and back this morning."

"Sure did." Cody absentmindedly ran his toy car along his bed rail.

"All right. No need to keep you in here when you should be opening presents at home tomorrow. I'll get the paperwork done so you can get out of here."

Kristi rubbed Cody's leg as the doctor walked out of the room, her smile so wide it almost hurt. They'd watched him closely in the week since the abduction, but there had been no ill effects except a nightmare. But she'd had plenty of those herself.

"Looking forward to being at home?"

He nodded. "And to presents."

Her stomach dropped. Presents. She hadn't had time to comb her hair more than twice since his surgery two weeks ago, let alone go shopping. The last time they'd been to the mall, they'd been chased by Loughlin's thugs. Picking out gifts hadn't been a priority when they were running for their lives.

They didn't have to run anymore.

But they also didn't have any presents.

"I'm sorry, bud. I don't have anything for you to open tomorrow."

Cody's face screwed up like he was thinking hard, and finally he nodded. "We can hang stockings with Zach tonight."

She nodded, trying to give him a genuine smile. "Stockings with Zach. Absolutely." But Zach was a bit of a wild card. She hadn't seen much of him in the week since he rescued them. His presence hovered around them just outside of view, tangible in a blanket laid over her while she slept and a new video game for Cody. Meals arrived and flowers filled vases. But Zach didn't appear.

And he didn't explain why.

"We can open presents with Zach next Christmas."

Oh, her sweet boy. She patted his knee and bit her quivering lips as the truth hit her hard. Best to begin preparing him now, begin preparing herself. "Bud, we might not be with Zach next Christmas."

Because he might not want them around.

He'd done everything he'd said he would. And now he was free to return to the life he wanted.

Cody screwed up his face again, but this time he couldn't come up with any understanding for her words. "Why not?"

"Well." She dragged the word out, hoping for a flash of brilliance. But there was none. "It's complicated."

"But you love him."

"Yes." She loved him. Of that she was sure.

"And he loves us." That part was less certain to her, despite Cody's confident pronouncement. Zach cared. Definitely. He had to. But love? Lifetime commitments? Those were things he hadn't promised.

"So why not tell him we'll be here for Christmas next year?"

From the mouths of babes.

Why not, indeed? She rummaged for any reason not to tell him that she wanted to stay. What did she have to lose? She was already broken. His rejection—even spoken aloud—couldn't tear her heart into any more pieces. She was already going to have to move out and move on.

It couldn't hurt anything but her pride to tell him the truth.

She'd do it.

But the minute he showed up in the doorway to take them home, she changed her mind. He looked so solemn, almost sad. The light in his eyes and half smile she'd come to love were gone, replaced by hard lines and stiff expressions.

She didn't know how to read this version of Zach. She couldn't look into his face and see what she needed to see.

But what if it was her last chance?

Zach drove them in silence, the traffic conspiring to get them home—to get them to *his* home—in record time. The early sunset had just begun to cast its glow over the city as he pulled into the driveway, scooped Cody from the backseat and led the way to the front door.

Kristi stumbled over her own feet, wondering how many more times they'd share this routine. How many more times would Cody hang over Zach's shoulder and hug his neck? How many chances would she have to thank him? So far, she hadn't taken even one. It was past time for that to change.

"Thank you." She blurted it out as he reached for the door handle, and he stopped with his hand still on the knob.

"For what?" He sounded genuinely surprised and also a little confused.

"For taking care of us. For finding us. For saving us." Tears formed in her eyes, and for the first time, she was embarrassed for him to see them. Ducking her head, she swiped them away, but they just kept coming.

He watched her for a long while, his gaze heavy but not chilling or frightening. It was warm and sincere like his embrace.

All she wanted was to trade places with her son, to be in Zach's arms, comforted and loved. She couldn't find the words to tell him, and the tears wouldn't stop and she hated that she was falling apart.

His eyebrows jumped as she brushed past him, but she tried not to notice as she barreled into the house, threw her purse down and stopped in her tracks.

"Merry Christmas."

She couldn't gasp in a breath to reply, not when she was faced with the magnificence he'd created in their living room. It wasn't just Christmas. It was Cody's Christmas.

A six-foot tree filled the room with fresh pine scent, twinkling white lights reflecting off brightly painted Corvette ornaments. Eight tiny Matchbox cars pulled a red sleigh across the top of the piano. Tinsel and garland were wrapped around every banister and hung over every arch. And beneath the tree were boxes and boxes of presents. All wrapped in paper adorned with sports cars.

"I hoped he'd make it home in time for Christmas." Zach set the sleeping boy down on the couch and tucked his favorite blanket around him.

And then she couldn't stop the tears from flowing down her face and dripping off her chin. She sniffed against her runny nose and hiccuped a sob.

"Hey." He tugged on her hand and pulled her in front of the tree. "What's wrong? Don't you like it?"

"It—it's perfect."

That half smile, the one where just one corner of his mouth lifted, appeared as he caught one of her tears with the pad of his thumb. "Then why are you crying?"

She tried for a stabilizing breath but settled for another wobbling sob. Then her words, like her tears, couldn't be held back. "I don't know. You've just been so good to us. And you rescued us. And you didn't have to."

He shook his head like he disagreed, but she didn't let him cut in. Not yet. Not while she was on a roll.

"And I didn't mean to. I didn't think I would. I didn't think I was ready. But then you were *you*, and I just... I fell in love." The word fell out of her mouth and lifted the weight off her shoulders at the same time. Sudden relief made her lighter than the tinsel hanging on the tree. But Zach looked so stunned that she decided to specify. "With you. I fell in love with you."

He started shaking his head again, his eyebrows pinched tight. "No."

Well, that hurt. She hunched her shoulders against the verbal blow.

"I'm not what you want," he argued. "I'm not soft-spoken or gentle. I'm always going to be that 'tough guy' who fights through the pain and refuses to spend a night in the hospital. For as long as I can, I'm going to serve my country, and my job isn't for the sweet or kind. I get called away on a moment's notice. I can't always be there for you. My life isn't particularly stable or serene."

He kept going, but she slowly tuned him out, rolling his words around until they made sense. He didn't say he didn't love her back. He just thought he wasn't what she wanted. What she needed.

In that thick skull of his, he'd convinced himself that she wanted someone else.

Someone like Aaron.

Hope bubbled deep in her chest, drying her tears and wiping the frown from her face.

She wasn't looking to replace Aaron. She was looking for Zach.

"Don't you see? I can't be what you want."

Now it was her turn to shake her head, only she gave him a full-blown smile as she did so. Snagging both of his hands, she squeezed them in front of her, praying she could convey all of the love in her heart.

"Zach McCloud, I disagree. Completely." One of his eyebrows rose, but he didn't interrupt her. "You may be all those things—rough-and-tumble, handy in a fight, called away at any moment. And maybe I didn't want those things when I was younger. But you've proven to be everything I never knew I needed."

He sucked in a quick gasp, and she giggled.

This was both harder and more wonderful than she'd hoped.

"You've been beside us through all of this. Any other man might have run, might have decided we weren't worth the effort."

"Never."

Her insides turned to mush, and she brought his hand to her heart, so he could feel it gallop. "You are the most stable man I know. You stand beside your convictions. You sacrifice for those you love. You never once got angry with me for not doing my own dishes."

That made him laugh, and he pulled her a step closer. She went willingly, craning her neck so she could see the lights dancing across his face.

"I didn't know I was ready to fall in love again, but

you made it so easy. And I want to spend next Christmas and the next and the next with you."

With a quick tug, he pulled her all the way against him, wrapping his arms around her waist. "That was my line."

"It was?"

"Uh-huh." He nodded into her hair. "I was going to tell you that I've been in love with you since we were sixteen."

"You were?" His confession was somehow infinitely surprising and not at all stunning. He'd been a good friend. And he'd always cared.

"But I never knew I could love someone this much until I married you."

Suddenly his embrace fell away, and she opened her eyes to find him kneeling before her. His hand rested on one knee, and he looked up at her with a playful grin. "Kristi McCloud, will you marry me?"

She shoved his shoulder to cover the tears that had returned. Her perfect proposal. Third time was a charm, they said.

"We're already married, silly."

"Let's make it real this time."

She fell into his arms and pressed her lips to his. "I think it already is."

EPILOGUE

Five months later

The back door slammed behind Zach as he carried a tray of hamburgers from the grill to the countertop.

"You can set them there." From her position in front of the sink, Kristi nodded toward the open spot between a plate of lettuce leaves and tomato slices and a bowl of fruit salad.

He did as she asked, sliding the still-sizzling meat into the buffet line before slipping up behind her and wrapping his arms around her waist.

"Hey." If she was trying to sound affronted, she failed miserably. Pressing a kiss to her neck, he laughed when she shivered.

"You shouldn't do that," she scolded.

"And why not?" He'd been waiting way too long to be free to kiss her and hold her and love her as he did now. He had no intention of wasting any more time.

With a tip of her head toward the backyard, she rolled her eyes. "We have company."

So what? He didn't particularly want an audience, but he wasn't bothered by letting his family see how much he loved his wife. Besides, everyone else was in the backyard. Cody and Jordan. Matt and Ashley. Tristan and Staci and all of their kids. And the rest of the guys from the team would be by soon enough. The adults were sipping lemonade and sitting in the shade. Well, all of them except Jordan, who had been chasing Cody and Tristan's oldest, Whitney, with a water gun last Zach had checked.

"They're outside. We're inside. Besides, you're my wife."

Her cheeks glowed pink as she turned in his arms, wrapping her own around his waist and holding him close. "I like it when you call me that."

"What, wife?"

She nodded.

He liked it, too. He liked that she was no longer his wife in name only. He liked that they'd committed before God and friends and family to love and honor one another, to care for one another, to stay together forever.

He liked the idea of forever.

Especially where Kristi was concerned.

Because she was going to own his heart at least that long.

Pressing his nose into her hair, he breathed in her scent. She smelled of honeysuckle and sunshine and the icing on Cody's birthday cake.

"I like that you're my wife."

"Me, too."

A scream of glee from outside made her jump, and he squeezed until she giggled. "That man likes hanging out with Cody because he can act like a kid."

"True. Although Jordan's never needed an excuse to act like a kid." But he had been spending an awful lot of time at Casa McCloud over the last few months. "Maybe he just hangs around because he likes the good food."

She pinched his arm playfully, and he jumped like she'd seriously injured him. Laughing, she said, "Maybe he's lonely. We should set him up."

"No." The word popped out before he could even register where it came from. But with it came a host of memories. The tremble in Amy's voice when Zach told her Jordan wasn't coming for their date. The coolness in her eyes the next time he saw her. The awkward silences when they'd met up.

All over a date that hadn't even been his to break.

"The last time someone set Jordan up on a date, it did not go well. So I'm staying out of that."

She wrinkled her nose, like she might have a better idea. "Maybe I know someone."

"Don't even think about it. Just let him play with the kids."

Something flashed in her eyes. But her bangs were in the way, and he wondered if he'd imagined it. Brushing her hair back with both hands, he leaned in until their noses were nearly touching. "What are you thinking, wife?"

Her eyes darted toward the backyard and the sounds of water balloons and children's laughter. "What would you think if there was another kid for Jordan to play with?"

His mind tumbled the words together but couldn't make much sense of them. "Do you want to have a baby?"

She bit into her bottom lip. "We haven't really talked about it, but…"

It was true. They hadn't talked about it. They'd had other things to worry about like getting Cody healthy, navigating life as a real married couple and feeding Jordan half the time.

Babies were a life changer. They came with late nights and endless dirty diapers, midnight feedings and scattered toys. Dirty dishes in his sink would be the least of his worries if they added a baby to the mix.

But he wasn't opposed to the idea. Especially not if it was a little girl with her mother's smile.

"When you're ready to talk about it, I'm open."

Suddenly tears filled her eyes, and he frowned. He'd said the wrong thing. Whatever that was.

"Kristi? Honey? What's—"

She shook her head and began to cry in earnest. "I'm pregnant."

He couldn't think. He couldn't move. He couldn't speak.

He must have stood like that for a long time because finally she nudged him. "Zach, say something. Are you mad?"

"Mad?" His legs shook, and suddenly he dropped to his knees, pressing his ear against her stomach and pulling her to him. "Mad?"

That wasn't even in the same galaxy as the emotions flooding through him. Joy. Elation.

Wonder.

That was closer.

There was a baby. And it was his. And Kristi's.

It felt like a kick in the chest followed by the warmest hug he'd ever known.

The life he'd wanted—the one he'd begged God for all those years ago—had been given to him. When God deemed the time to be right.

Turning his head, he nuzzled her belly and pressed a kiss to the place where their baby grew as she cupped each side of his head and forced him to look up at her.

"Tell me the truth. Are you happy?"

Clearing the lump from his throat, he hunted for the words. "*Happy* doesn't begin to cover it. I'm married to the love of my life, we have an amazing son and we're going to have another one."

"It might be a girl."

He kissed her stomach again, pressing his hands to each side and imagining what it would be like to feel their baby kick and watch it grow. "I didn't even know I wanted to have a baby until now. But I've only ever wanted one thing as much."

"To be on the teams?"

He frowned. "No. You."

She laughed and leaned over, pressing her lips to his and promising him a future filled with as much joy, laughter and love as they could squeeze into it.

* * * * *

Don't miss these other MEN OF VALOR
stories from Liz Johnson:

*A PROMISE TO PROTECT
SEAL UNDER SIEGE
NAVY SEAL NOEL
NAVY SEAL SECURITY*

Find more great reads at www.LoveInspired.com.

Dear Reader,

Thank you for joining Zach, Kristi and me on this adventure. I hope you enjoyed reading their story as much as I enjoyed writing it.

Zach appeared in the first Men of Valor book, *A Promise to Protect*, and he's been waiting not-so-patiently for his own story ever since. In fact, he's been waiting for a lot of things, especially Kristi. I love how he's willing to sacrifice his own happiness for hers. And I love that his sacrifice begins to open her eyes to a love she never expected.

Both Zach and Kristi—and even Cody—get second chances at the right time. I've never been one who likes to wait, but Zach and Kristi remind me that God's timing is perfect. I hope when you feel like God hasn't heard you or that you can't possibly wait any longer, this story will remind you that everything has a season and God's timing is best.

Thanks for spending your time with us. I'd love to hear from you. You can reach me at liz@lizjohnsonbooks.com, Twitter.com/LizJohnsonBooks or Facebook.com/LizJohnsonBooks. Or visit LizJohnsonBooks.com to sign up for my newsletter.

Liz Johnson

REQUEST YOUR FREE BOOKS!

2 FREE RIVETING INSPIRATIONAL NOVELS
PLUS 2 FREE MYSTERY GIFTS

Love Inspired
SUSPENSE
RIVETING INSPIRATIONAL ROMANCE

YES! Please send me 2 FREE Love Inspired® Suspense novels and my 2 FREE mystery gifts (gifts are worth about $10). After receiving them, if I don't wish to receive any more books, I can return the shipping statement marked "cancel." If I don't cancel, I will receive 4 brand-new novels every month and be billed just $4.99 per book in the U.S. or $5.49 per book in Canada. That's a savings of at least 17% off the cover price. It's quite a bargain! Shipping and handling is just 50¢ per book in the U.S. and 75¢ per book in Canada.* I understand that accepting the 2 free books and gifts places me under no obligation to buy anything. I can always return a shipment and cancel at any time. Even if I never buy another book, the two free books and gifts are mine to keep forever.

123/323 IDN GH5Z

Name _____ (PLEASE PRINT)

Address _____ Apt. #

City _____ State/Prov. _____ Zip/Postal Code

Signature (if under 18, a parent or guardian must sign)

Mail to the **Reader Service:**
IN U.S.A.: P.O. Box 1867, Buffalo, NY 14240-1867
IN CANADA: P.O. Box 609, Fort Erie, Ontario L2A 5X3

Are you a current subscriber to Love Inspired® Suspense books
and want to receive the larger-print edition?
Call 1-800-873-8635 or visit www.ReaderService.com.

* Terms and prices subject to change without notice. Prices do not include applicable taxes. Sales tax applicable in N.Y. Canadian residents will be charged applicable taxes. Offer not valid in Quebec. This offer is limited to one order per household. Not valid for current subscribers to Love Inspired Suspense books. All orders subject to credit approval. Credit or debit balances in a customer's account(s) may be offset by any other outstanding balance owed by or to the customer. Please allow 4 to 6 weeks for delivery. Offer available while quantities last.

Your Privacy—The Reader Service is committed to protecting your privacy. Our Privacy Policy is available online at www.ReaderService.com or upon request from the Reader Service.

We make a portion of our mailing list available to reputable third parties that offer products we believe may interest you. If you prefer that we not exchange your name with third parties, or if you wish to clarify or modify your communication preferences, please visit us at www.ReaderService.com/consumerschoice or write to us at Reader Service Preference Service, P.O. Box 9062, Buffalo, NY 14240-9062. Include your complete name and address.

LIS15

SPECIAL EXCERPT FROM

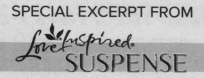

*When an ordinary trip into the Montana mountains
leads to a deadly game of cat and mouse, can
wilderness expert Zane Scofield protect himself and
Heather Jacobs…or will his dangerous past doom them
both?*

Read on for a sneak preview of
BIG SKY SHOWDOWN
by **Sharon Dunn**, *available January 2017 from
Love Inspired Suspense!*

Zane Scofield stared through his high-powered binoculars,
scanning the hills and mountains all around him. For the
last day or so, he'd had the strange sense that they were
being watched. Who had been stalking them and why?

He saw movement through his binoculars and focused
in. Several ATVs were headed down the mountain toward
the campsite where he'd left Heather alone. He zeroed in
and saw the handmade flag. He knew that flag. His mind
was sucked back in time seven years ago to when he had
lived in these mountains as a scared seventeen-year-old.
If this was who he thought it was, Heather was in danger.

He could hear the ATVs drawing closer, but not coming
directly into the camp. They were headed a little deeper
into the forest. He ran toward the mechanical sound,
pushing past the rising fear.

He called for Heather only once. He stopped to listen.

He heard her call back—faint and far away, repeating his name. He ran in the direction of the sound with his rifle still slung over his shoulder. When he came to the clearing, he saw a boy not yet in his teens throwing rocks into a hole and screaming, "Shut up. Be quiet."

Zane held his rifle up toward the boy. He could never shoot a child, but maybe the threat would be enough.

The kid grew wide-eyed and snarled at him. "More men are coming. So there." Then the boy darted into the forest, yelling behind him, "You won't get away."

Zane ran over to the hole. Heather gazed up at him, relief spreading across her face.

Voices now drifted through the trees, men on foot headed this way.

Zane grabbed an evergreen bough and stuck it in the hole for Heather to grip. She climbed agilely and quickly. He grabbed her hand and pulled her the rest of the way out. "We have to get out of here."

There was no time to explain the full situation to her. His worst nightmare coming true, his past reaching out to pull him into a deep dark hole. The past he thought he'd escaped.

If Willis was back in the high country, he needed to get Heather to safety and fast. He knew what Willis was capable of. Their lives depended on getting out of the high country.

Don't miss
BIG SKY SHOWDOWN
by Sharon Dunn, available wherever
Love Inspired® Suspense books and ebooks are sold.

www.LoveInspired.com

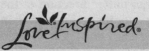
*A promise to watch out for his late army buddy's
little brother might have this single rancher in over
his head. But he's not the only one who wants to
care for the boy...*

Read on for a sneak preview of the fourth book in the
LONE STAR COWBOY LEAGUE: BOYS RANCH
miniseries, **THE COWBOY'S TEXAS FAMILY**
by **Margaret Daley**.

As Nick settled behind the steering wheel and started his
truck, he slanted a look at Darcy. "So what do you think
about the boys ranch?"

"Corey is much better off here than with his dad. He's
not happy right now, but then he wasn't happy at home."

"He's scared." That was why Bea had brought him to
the barn first to see Nick. "He'll feel better after he meets
some of the other boys his age."

"What if he doesn't?" Darcy asked.

"He's confused. He wants to be with his dad, and yet
not if he's always being left alone. He doesn't know what
to expect from day to day and certainly doesn't feel safe."
Those same feelings used to plague Nick while he was
growing up.

"I've dealt with kids like that."

"In a perfect world, Ned wouldn't drink and would
love Corey unconditionally. But that isn't going to hap-

pen. Ned isn't going to change." He knew firsthand the mind-set of an alcoholic and remembered the times his dad promised to stop drinking and reform. He never did; in fact he got worse.

"How do you know that for sure?"

"I just do." He didn't share his past with anyone. It was a part of his life he wanted to wipe from his mind, but it was always there in the background. He never wanted to see a child grow up the way he had.

"Then I'll pray for the best for Corey," Darcy said.

"The best scenario would be the state taking Corey away from Ned and a good family adopting him. I wish I was in a position to do it." The second he said that last sentence he wanted to snatch it back. He had no business being anyone's father.

"Because you're single? That might not matter in certain cases."

"I'm not dad material." How could he explain that he was struggling to erase the debt that his father had accumulated? If he lost the ranch, he would lose his home and job. But, more important, what if he wasn't a good father to Corey? It was one thing to be there to help when needed, but it was very different to be totally responsible for raising a child.

Don't miss
THE COWBOY'S TEXAS FAMILY
by Margaret Daley, available January 2017 wherever
Love Inspired® books and ebooks are sold.

www.LoveInspired.com